A Place Within Her

D.P. McHenry

Throw Me A Kiss Publishing
ISBN: 9780990695936

To Jet and Trevor, my Caribbean posse, with thanks.

Table of Contents

ONE

Thea waited until the sun hung low enough over the horizon to look like it was melting into the ocean before starting to shoot. These were the photos that post card buyers sought out, as mind numbing as she thought they were, tourists wanted the quintessential Caribbean sunset. They sold, and she made money. Enough to keep her afloat here on Nevis, and along with her wedding photography that money allowed her to do what she really loved, which was draw. Her drawings were in some of the local galleries, and on St. Kitts and St. Maarten, but it would be awhile before she could make a living solely on those. And who knew how long she would remain in Nevis. Her background was in sales so she knew how to market her own stuff, the problem was she marketed the boring stuff too well and ended up with a lot of weddings and guesthouse brochure photo gigs. It paid the bills. She didn't live extravagantly; she rented a studio apartment from her friends who owned The Figtree Inn for a reduced rate. She turned an indigenous Caribbean hut into a photo lab; the deal was she would do any photo work they needed for free and she'd have the run of the place. Most of the weddings she photographed were there, as they had one of the most beautiful spots on the island. But for now she was at the far end of Pinney's Beach, quietly perched in a coconut palm that had been toppled by the last hurricane, waiting for the perfect shot. Her vantage point gave her a great view, and the fig tree leaves made a beautiful frame for her shots. A man came running down the beach.

"Great," she thought, "he decides to exercise in the middle of my lens at the precise 1/100th of a second I could make a few bucks."

His long legs seemed to glide effortlessly over the hard packed sand. He was tall, over 6', with hair the color of the beach. It looked like he was a blond going gray. His green running shorts were the color of the water at this time of day. He was very well put together, a point not lost on Thea. Well muscled but not bulging, his long and lean form reminded her of a swimmer. He stopped and looked out over the water, bent over with his hands on his knees, catching his breath. She snapped several photos of him, though she was not sure why. He couldn't see her; she was hidden from his view by the fig trees. He stood up and ran his hands through his hair. She continued to shoot, getting close-ups of his face. It was a classically handsome face, with a chiseled chin and strong cheekbones, and a long straight nose. He looked about 45 or so. His eyes were blue or maybe gray, the reflected water made them look translucent. The face was sad. More than sad, really; in despair was a better description. He closed his eyes and clenched his fists. She shot more frames as he waded into the calm surf and splashed water on his face. She watched as he turned back toward her and paced back and forth.

"This is a mind in torment," she thought to herself.

Thea saw a launch in the distance headed in this direction from the south, and two men walking down the beach from the other direction.

"Did somebody send out invitations? This end of the beach you don't see this much action in high season!" she thought.

She shot more photos to prove to Irene back at the Inn that there really were that many people on Pinney's Beach at the same time. Not to mention the two guys walking this way looked more like they were on their way to a mall in New Jersey, not walking a

Caribbean beach. Irene would never believe it. All that polyester must be really toasty.

Just then things got interesting. The Polyester boys walked by the runner, who glanced at them over his shoulder. Before they passed him they turned and jumped him, one grabbing his arms and the other landing a blow to his stomach. Thea felt adrenaline shoot through her body and at the same time she thought she'd vomit. She was terrified. In one horrific moment she was out of her perch, the camera was on the ground somewhere and she was running full steam at these two guys. The one holding the runner's arms didn't see it coming when she side kicked him in the kidneys. He made a horrible coughing sound and dropped to his knees. She'd never thought Tae Bo would be useful. Freed, the runner swung at the other guy and connected with his jaw. The guy on his knees grabbed Thea as she was attempting to land another kick and pushed her away, sending her sprawling on her back. By that time the launch was almost on shore, and three very large men came flying at this melee. Outnumbered, the polyester boys got up and ran as fast as they could. Two of the men from the launch grabbed the runner and threw him into the vessel, as the third shoved off from shore. Thea got to her knees and could see the runner bent over, holding his gut and coughing as one of them handed him a towel. He was gesturing what looked like a signal to go back. The one steering shook his head as the launch continued back the way it came.

"Chivalry is most definitely dead," she thought. "Help a guy out of a jam and he doesn't even say thank you, never mind offer you a lift home."

Thea stood up and was dizzy. She was suddenly afraid the polyester boys would come back. She ran to the palm tree and fished around for her camera, shooing away a gecko. She threw the camera over her shoulder and headed for the path. It was almost dark and she walked quietly, trying to listen for anyone else around. She made it to the mini Moke without incident, thanked the Universe once more when it started on the first try, and sped off toward the Figtree Inn, her heart pounding out of her chest.

TWO

Jett was standing in the kitchen doorway as Thea pulled her Moke into the employee car park. Dinner would be in full swing. Wednesday, which meant a steel band was entertaining on the patio. Sometimes if the crowd seemed particularly dull Irene would beg Thea to come to dinner and help liven things up. Jett waved her over as she got out of the Moke.

"Miss Irene asked that you come in for dessert," he said. His look changed from amused to concerned when he saw Thea's face, and the sand all over her clothes and hat.

"Jett, tell Irene I can't tonight…"

"What happened?" Jett had been an employee at Figtree since he was 13. He was now 25 and a graduate of Johnson & Wales' Hotel Management School, and working on his beloved island until he could save enough to open his own restaurant. He was Thea's biggest fan when after a trip to Nevis 10 years ago she returned to Boston and sent him a book on napkin folding. The handsome young black man had a blaze of a birthmark across his temple. When he was 15 he admitted to being self-conscious about it, so Thea told him that God marked the special ones, and that he should be happy to have a personal paint job from the Almighty. He wore it proudly from then on. He thought of himself as Thea's personal guardian when she came to live on Nevis two years ago. Her present condition made him very unhappy.

"Oh, Jett, it's a long story, and I'll need to tell Irene and Sam as well, so when the guests are finished dessert and make their way to the patio I'll come down to the great room and tell it once. OK?"

She kissed his cheek.

"Are you alright?"

"A little shaken up. I need a shower. Tell Irene and Sam I'll be down in half an hour."

He nodded and she walked up the steps past the sweet smell of the chalice vine growing next to her room. Once the light was on she checked on her camera. There was a nice ding in the side of her old Leica, but it looked purely cosmetic so she used her air blower to brush a little sand away and put the camera in her safe. She kept all her equipment in there anyway, but she was uncomfortable about leaving any stuff around tonight. The incident shook her up, even though she didn't think anyone saw her taking any pictures. Hell, other than the guy she kicked she wasn't sure anyone knew she was there at all!

She felt better after the shower. She threw on a sundress and flip-flops and made her way to the great room. Jett followed her in with her favorite grilled cheese and chutney sandwich on raisin bread, and Sam took one look at her and poured her a large Maker's Mark on the rocks. She smiled at them both.

"Jett, I am definitely going to devour that, but I really need the stuff in the glass first," she said. Jett chuckled as he put down the sandwich on the cocktail table. Thea took a deep swallow of bourbon and plunked herself down into the soft cushions of the couch. Irene came mamboing in to the music of the steel band, making them all laugh. Thea realized how happy these people made her.

Irene and Sam were expatriates who hailed from Philadelphia. Sam's work at Barclay's Bank brought them to the Caribbean, and when they saw the run down old Figtree Inn, they decided to give it a go. The rest, as they say, is history. Thea had been a regular Figtree guest for a while, coming every year to escape the New England winters. She and Irene kept in touch, and when Thea's life was turned upside down Irene and Sam welcomed her with open arms, and she decided to stay.

"What's going on, hon?" Irene asked.

Thea recounted the story to the three of them, and Jett moved to the sofa and took her hand.

"Jett, I'm OK, really," she tried to get him to look less concerned. Sam piped in.

"What if those goons look for you? There aren't many tourists on the island in July, and you're the only redheaded permanent resident. I think we need to call Peter..."

Thea rolled her eyes and rested her head on the back of the couch. Peter Moses was the police chief on the island, and was also Jett's half brother.

"That really isn't necessary..." she began. Irene cut her off.

"Sam, you're right, that red hair would tip them off. Thea, you're not safe. I can't believe that thoughtless idiot left you on the beach by yourself!"

"But..." Thea tried to interject.

"I think we need to get a hold of Peter right now," Sam continued.

"They didn't see her hair." Everyone looked at Jett. "She was wearing a baseball cap."

"THANK YOU, Jett. That's what I've been trying to tell you. It was getting dark, I had my hat on with all my hair up underneath it and I never said anything. I doubt they'd recognize me. It all happened too fast." She paused. "I'd recognize them though."

"How, by the polyester?" Sam asked.

"No, I have pictures." She grinned. "I'll develop them tomorrow and take them to Peter myself. If we're lucky, the thugs are gone by now, and so is Prince Charming, and we won't have to worry about it at all."

They seemed somewhat satisfied that no one would come looking for Thea that night, so Sam and Irene said they wouldn't call Peter, and Thea could see him tomorrow and give a full report. She finished the last delicious morsel of her sandwich, and gave each of her protectors a kiss on the cheek, bidding them good night. Thea walked up the stairs again, this time stopping to pick a Chalice Vine flower for her pillow. She inhaled deeply recalling a happy memory. She left her door open so she could hear the steel band on the patio, and sat at her desk. She wrote about today's incident in her journal while it was fresh in her mind; this was a bit more exciting than the most recent entries about tides and hummingbirds. It also brought back the scared feelings she'd finally thought she'd gotten over. Her entries had gradually become more mundane after 22 months of soul searching since her arrival. She was actually feeling pretty spiritually and emotionally healthy again.

Thea had been a well respected and highly paid Division Manager for a grower's cooperative back in Boston. She traveled a great deal, negotiated advertising and promotions with supermarkets and mass merchandisers, and managed a network of direct sales people in the Northeast Corridor. She liked her job and the people she worked with, she had a nice home in Winchester, just outside of Boston, and a long time lover to whom she felt a strong connection. They never married, there seemed to be no point. She didn't want kids, he had one from a previous marriage who hung out with them on weekends, so they just chose to live together and save all the paperwork and hassle of a wedding. They traveled a lot with all her frequent flyer miles, and had a fun life. Kip, her lover, was a researcher at a medical facility in Cambridge, and Donny, his son, lived in Lexington with his mother. Thea, Kip and Donny were close, and Kip had an amiable relationship with his ex wife, which made it easier on all of them. Donny liked Thea, and traveled with the couple pretty regularly. The year he was 17 Thea and Kip mused how they wouldn't be seeing very much of him anymore as he'd discovered girls and had a car. But Donny was pretty much a regular at their house, even bringing a date occasionally, as he just really liked being around them.

Thea's parents lived in Newburyport, and they loved having Thea's 'family' visit on occasional summer weekends. They would go out to Plum Island to swim, or walk around town and shop. Kip took Donny and Thea's dad Tom fishing on a charter once or twice as well. But in the winter of 1996 things began to change. Thea's mom, Frances, had been complaining that Tom had been getting forgetful, and that it had been getting worse over the winter. Thea spoke to her folks once a week on the phone, and saw them once a month or so in the winter, but hadn't really noticed a big change in her dad. Partly because she spoke to her mother more often, and partly because her dad always wanted to know where she'd been and what she'd been doing, so she did most of the talking. He asked a few questions occasionally that she thought she'd already answered, but she let it slide, thinking she probably just wasn't paying enough attention. She was normally making dinner or doing something else when she spoke to them.

In February her father was diagnosed with Alzheimer's. The doctors were trying a radical therapy to diminish the symptoms, but as part of a clinical test the side effects were not totally known. Her parents, her mother actually, decided she'd risk anything to have her old husband back. Thea wasn't prepared for the frantic call from her mother in April.

"Thea!" her mother was crying. "You need to come home right away! He's crazy, Thea!"

"Mom, calm down. What's going on, who's crazy?"

"Your father! He's ranting and raving and threatening me. I'm in the bedroom with the door locked." Her mother was sobbing.

"What happened?"

"I haven't told you, I didn't know how to tell you! I was waiting to see you."

"Mom, for christsakes, what!"

"It's the drugs they gave him for the Alzheimer's. The doctor said this might happen but the chances were slim. The doctor told me all these things, Thea. Told me about the progression if the drugs fail, how they get angry! And sometimes there's dementia! Oh, dear God, I didn't think it would happen so soon!"

"Mom, I'll call the police, and I'll be there as soon as I can."

"No, Thea, not the police!"

"Mom, if you can't reason with him and he's angry, he could hurt you." By this time Thea was crying, too. "He needs to be restrained. He's a big guy, mom, I'm afraid for you."

She could hear his deep voice screaming as he banged on the bedroom door.

"Mom, don't open that door! Where is his gun?" Thea hated that he had one, but he pooh-poohed her concerns years ago saying it was for their safety. She hadn't even remembered it until now.

"It's in here, with me." She was whispering.

"Mom, I'm calling the police, I'll be right there."
She hung up and dialed directory assistance for
Newburyport. She told the operator it was an
emergency and they patched her through. She explained
the situation and the 911 operator assured her there
would be an officer there in minutes. She jumped in the
car and sped toward her parents' home, knowing it
would be 45 minutes if she drove like a maniac and
didn't get stopped by the police. She pressed the speed
dial on her cell phone for her mother and it began to
ring. It just rang and rang, no one picked up. She let it
ring until the recording came on to tell her no one was
answering. Brilliant fucking deduction. She hit redial
and tried again. This happened all the way up Rt. 93. On
Rt. 95 north, she got the recording again. By Danvers
she was frantic. She tried one last time. It continued to
ring as she passed the exit for Topsfield, and as she saw
the signs for Rowley someone picked up the receiver.

"Hello!" she screamed, "Is anyone there?"

"Who is this?" asked a man's voice.

"Who is this?" she asked. "I'm Thea Garrett, Tom
and Frances Garrett's daughter."

"Oh, well, Miss Garrett, I'm Officer Vale of the
Newburyport Police. Are you on your way?"

"Yes, I'm about 5 minutes out. Is everything
alright?"

"It's best if we speak with you in person, Miss
Garrett."

"WHAT HAPPENED? Tell me!" she screamed. At
that point she was screeching around the corner and
onto their street. There were 3 police cruisers with
flashing lights outside the house, along with an
ambulance. Neighbors were gathered outside of the
gate, and her parents' good friends from next-door, Bob

and Nancy, were crying. They saw Thea running toward the house; Bob grabbed her.

"No, Thea, don't go in." His look of horror made her heart drop to her feet. Conversely, her stomach felt as though it was forcing it's way up and into her throat. She pushed past him. A police officer stopped her.

"I'm Althea Garrett. What happened?" The officer motioned to a detective, who took her aside to the breezeway by the garage for privacy. Thea didn't really remember what happened next, all she could recall was screaming and crying and trying to hit the police detective as an EMT ran over to assist him. The sedative they gave her almost knocked her off her feet, and the next thing she remembered was sitting on the stoop with a cup of water, trying to make sense of what she'd just heard, the detective sitting next to her. She rose unsteadily, walked into the back yard and vomited next to the garden shed. She leaned against it for support, and heard the detective's words ring in her ears:

"Your father was able to put his hands on a gun in the house. He shot and killed your mother, and then turned the weapon on himself."

She threw up again. Both her parents were dead. How could two seemingly normal, healthy 70 year-old people be gone? Like this? She started to weep.

Eventually Kip came to get her. She didn't know how long she'd been there or even who had called him. She was in a daze. Bob and Nancy were sitting with her holding her hand. The parish priest came and had a few words with her, talking about God's way. She was too stunned to respond, but all she could think was how can a loving and caring God allow this to happen?

The next few weeks were hell on earth. She spoke with their doctor to try to understand why this happened, and Kip's colleagues tried to help her with her struggle to know. Their caskets were closed; she had been the only one to see them, but these weren't her parents. The shots had done so much damage.

"Mom, why did you open the door?"

The wake seemed never to end. People didn't know what to say, or how to ask what happened. Thea felt as bad for them as they did for her. Friends were wonderful, and took over her life so she could have time to heal. But the worst part was the cemetery. Thea didn't want to leave her parents there. She couldn't believe she would have to walk away and never see them again.

There was a reception at a local restaurant after the service, and people drifted off to their cars. Kip gave her a moment alone at the gravesite. Thea felt guilt. Had she not listened enough? Had she not been there? Could she have stopped this from happening? The prayer she said was not for their salvation, for if there was no salvation for two souls as good as Frances and Tom Garrett, then there was no God. Her prayer was for understanding. And forgiveness.

Thea hired a professional cleaning company to take care of the house, as she could not even go into it. She was thankful their lawyer was organized and efficient, and the processing of their estate did not take long. Her parents were not wealthy. They were living comfortably on their investments and social security, and Thea helped them out with the niceties whenever they mentioned they liked or needed something. She directed the lawyer to continue to invest her inheritance, and made a donation to an Alzheimer's research foundation in their names. She took some family things from the house after it had been cleaned, donated the rest to the Salvation Army, and sold the house quickly. Coming into summer it was an easy and profitable sale.

She eventually went back to work, but each day was a struggle. Her company was understanding, and gave her the flexible hours she needed to seek some therapy. She was going through all of the stages of grief, and while she outwardly understood the process, her insides were rebelling. Kip had been kind and generous, giving her space and being there for her when she needed him. Donny had been so sweet. He'd drop by on the nights he knew his father would be out late and stay with her so she wouldn't be alone. He'd make coffee for her and just sit with her and watch TV or listen to music.

One night while they were watching TV they saw flashing lights outside and got up to see what was going on. The sight of flashing lights made Thea slightly ill ever since her parents' deaths. Her knees went weak as the two officers ascended the steps to their front door. Donny could see her distress and asked the officers what was up.

"Are you Thea Garrett?" they asked her.

"Yes," she said quietly.

"I'm afraid there's been an accident."

"What?" Donny asked, "Who, my father?" The officers looked at the teenager.

"What's your name, son?" the older one asked.

"Donny Franklin." Thea was mute, and just closed her eyes and listened.

"Is Harris Franklin your father?"

"Yeah."

"I'm sorry, young man. I'm afraid your father was in a multi car accident on route 93 tonight, involving an S.U.V. and a tractor-trailer as well as his vehicle. He didn't make it."

Thea crushed her face into Donny's hair and hugged him as he wailed in misery. She could not believe this was happening. Not Kip, not after what had happened to her parents. Her misery and her anger turned into a crisis of faith. Thea held it together through Kip's funeral, and assisted Donny in dealing with the insurance money and settlement of Kip's estate. She was happy to see that Kip had provided well for his son's future, and had even left something in his will for Thea, although she had not expected much. She had told him long ago that his first priority was his son, and that she would be just fine. Well, he had made his son a priority, but she wasn't fine.

She slogged through the days and wondered what it was all about. Why was she being tested like this? Was this punishment for a badly lived previous life? What was her purpose here? No one had the answers, not the priest, not the shrink, not her friends or the bartender. All she had worked for and all she had accomplished were for what? It took almost a year of therapy, writing in her journal, meditating on her life and searching her soul. She decided that either you did all this for nothing or that the key was in understanding that each day was a gift to be savored not spent laboring toward a goal you might never reach. Her peace came in realizing that her parents had lived life that way. They really did stop to smell the roses, not waiting until retirement to have fun and begin their lives together. It gave her some measure of solace to realize that she and Kip had enjoyed what little time they'd had together, too. But now, her life didn't seem to fit anymore. She chose a radical approach; she chucked it all away.

Irene and Sam supported her idea of her photography business, and she had the money to rehab an indigenous Nevis house into a studio and lab on their property and to get started. She had minored in Photography in college and it had been her hobby ever since. She moved to the island in 1997 and had a modest income from her work and her inheritance, and did her best to be happy. Her true goal was to try to make the world a bit better through her actions.

When she finished her entry in her journal she wrote a letter to Donny. He would be going back to college soon, and he'd talked about coming to visit her next month. If he were coming, they'd need to make plans.

Peter Moses got out of his jeep and walked toward the kitchen door. Jett saw him coming and went out to meet him. Peter grabbed his younger brother and kissed his birthmark, while tousling his short braids. "You bastard." Jett jibed as he punched his arm.

"We share the same father and you call me a bastard?" Peter feigned incredulousness. "Hey, when are you going to make dinner for me?" he added.

Jett laughed. Peter jabbed his brother in the arm. "Where's T?" he asked. His accent was more British than Caribbean. Jett pointed up the stairs.

"Did you tell her you rang me up?"

"No." Jett said quietly. Peter smiled at him and shook his head.

He quickly mounted the stairs and stopped in the doorway. Thea was standing at her desk, checking a date book with some things on her bulletin board, her back to the door. The sundress she wore had spaghetti straps and a very low back. Her red hair skimmed her shoulders. He studied her. He had always loved that back. She protected herself from the sun, but it still turned her skin a golden color with an explosion of freckles. Her shoulders were beautiful as well. He loved that she felt like a woman in his arms, not a bunch of bones and skin. He wanted to walk over and kiss those freckles while he wound his arms around her waist. Based on the story Jett had told him and the way she undoubtedly felt she'd probably scream loud enough to be heard on Saba. He knocked gently on the doorframe. Even that made her jump. She turned to look at him. She chuckled and shook her head.

"Jett call you?" she asked. He smiled and nodded. She wasn't unhappy to see him. He was so great to look at that for that reason alone she was always glad to see him. She was used to seeing him about town in his starched, white, short-sleeved uniform. Tonight he had on khaki shorts and a black tee shirt. The outfit showed off his long muscled legs and great arms. He reminded her of the British actor Colin Salmon, with his hair cropped short, his cappuccino colored skin and beautiful green gray eyes, and those lips.

"What happened?" he asked.

Thea sighed audibly. She gestured for him to sit. He sat down on the bed and then relaxed into a reclining position on his elbow, head resting on his hand.

"You want a beer?" she asked.

"Yeah."

She reached into her mini fridge for a Red Stripe and handed it to him, sitting on the edge of the bed. She started telling him the story as he sipped the beer. He occasionally interrupted with a question.

"Can you describe the two men?"

"I have pictures."

He nodded. Of course she did, she photographed everything. He finished his beer and sat up to put the bottle on the nightstand. She continued speaking. He watched her shoulders hunch up with tension as she told the story. He could resist no longer, and began rubbing her back with his thumbs just above her shoulder blades. She didn't stop him. She described the attack and told him that she ran at the guy and kick boxed his kidneys.

"You did what?" he almost shouted. He was furious with her. She said nothing, and the shoulders started their upward migration again. He exhaled.

"You could have been seriously hurt or killed." His voice became gentle. His hands went her shoulders to her neck as he mocked strangling her. She finished telling the story. He turned her to face him, his hands on her shoulders still.

"Woman, you need to exercise some caution."

"They didn't see my face or my hair, I don't think."

"I mean in general."

"Oh. What happens now?"

"The attack hasn't been reported," he looked down at his beeper to be sure there was no missed call, "so I'd say someone is trying to keep it quiet. You said the launch wasn't from the big hotel, so I'd wager there is a yacht in the outer harbor. The parties involved may all be gone from the island by now. The water taxi to St. Kitts and two more flights left the airfield tonight after the time it happened. I want those photographs tomorrow, please."

She nodded.

"And I want you to be careful until I can investigate."

She nodded again.

"In the meantime I'll just have to protect you." She gave him a do-I-look-like-I-just-fell-off-a-turnip-truck look. He smiled. He turned her around and pulled her toward him so she sat between his legs. He began his work on her shoulders again, and as the tension eased she dropped her head to one side. Her hair drifted down, exposing the crook of her neck. He leaned forward and kissed her there, and gently bit her as his kisses worked down her back. The quiet sounds she made let him know his attentions were welcome. He pulled her against him, reaching for her chin and moving it toward his face. His lips brushed hers gently, then more hungrily, as he wrapped his arm around her and shifted her body to face his. His tongue probed hers, as he slipped her strap off her shoulder, exposing her breast. His hand cupped it, massaging her flesh as his thumb teased her nipple. Her moan told him to continue. He lay back on the bed, pulling her along side him. He pulled at her dress and slid it up and over her head, while she worked at unbuttoning his trousers. He shed his tee shirt, and slid the shorts and briefs to the floor in one motion. She raised her hips and let him remove her panties. He moved her legs apart and lay between them, kissing her breasts and making her ache with longing. She rubbed her pelvis against his thigh signaling that she wanted him, as his attentions to her nipples made her gasp. He rose up and slid into her, and she cried out. He paused and ran his fingers down her cheek.

"Are you alright?" he asked. She smiled at him, eyes half open, and nodded. He was always a surprise. She began to move her hips and he thrust to her rhythm. He felt the cheeks of her ass as he pulled her toward him, and moved to stroke her breasts. He could sense she was close to climax. He whispered to her.

"I've missed you, T. I've missed watching you come."

She lost control. The release made the tension in her shoulders turn to fiery crystals that flooded her body. She arched her back and grabbed his shoulders as she worked herself on his cock, not wanting the pleasure to end. It really did make him crazy to watch her, and he did miss it. He thrust harder to keep her ride going, but the beauty of her climax, the feeling he had watching her did him in. He came hard, the groan rising in his throat and turning to a gasp. His body sagged but he kept himself up on his arms. She rose up and kissed him, and he willingly let her pull him back down. They lay entwined until their breathing became normal again.

"Tell me again why we don't do this all the time?" he asked.

She laughed. She loved listening to his voice.

"Because as long as you're fucking me you'll never find that woman to marry who'll give you all those babies."

"Hmm. Perhaps I should reconsider the babies."

"Don't settle, Peter." She looked at his eyes when she spoke. "You don't love me. You love making love to me. We have an understanding, remember?"

"You're right," he said quietly. "This part is just so, bloody good." He caressed her as she lay in the crook of his arm.

Thea and Peter had been drawn to each other when they first met. Thea had been on the island for six months, and Peter had just accepted the position of chief after 10 years as a DCI in England. His father had sent him to England to be educated, and he had remained there after law school, but found police work more intriguing than being a barrister. His father, Abrahim Moses, was the lawyer on the island, and while disappointed that neither of his sons chose law, he always respected their decisions. Peter's mother died when he was a child, and Abrahim remarried a lovely woman from St. Kitts. Peter adored his stepmother, Callie, and doted on Jett who was 10 years his junior. He

25

missed Jett terribly when he went away to school, but Jett managed to travel to England several times to be with his big brother. Peter visited Jett at school in Rhode Island as well. Thea knew all about Peter, as Jett spoke of him often, and looked forward to meeting him. She expected another brother, she supposed, as she adored Jett as though he was the brother she never had, and Jett treated Thea as a much loved older sister. She hadn't expected the sparks. The day Peter interviewed and accepted his post as Chief of Police was a day of great celebration for the Moses family. Peter was coming home! Thea had been on Antigua the day he arrived and had not yet met him when the announcement was made. An impromptu party was called at the Figtree Inn. Even though it was high season and the Inn was full, the party was held and all the guests were invited. Actually, most of the island was invited. It was so like Irene and Sam to do such a thing. The guest of honor arrived with his father and stepmother, as Jett was heading up the kitchen staff that evening to prepare a feast that would not soon be forgotten. Thea was taking photographs of the island's families, some candid, some posed. At one point Jett caught her elbow and whispered to her. "My brother wants to meet you."

"Oh, good." She said as she looked around."If you've told him as much about me as you've told me about him I'm sure he's pretty curious, too."

"No, it's not like that." She looked at Jett. "I didn't say I wanted to introduce you. He saw you and said to me 'Who is she? I want to meet her.'"

Thea felt her face get red. She hadn't dated or been with anyone since Kip died. Now someone was interested? She didn't know what to think or how to behave. She smiled nervously at Jett. He pulled her by the hand through the crowd and out onto the patio. Peter was chatting with the racetrack manager and his wife, as the postmaster looked on. He looked up to see his brother with the gorgeous redhead he'd seen inside earlier.

"He's busy." Thea said, as she looked down and began to back away. Peter very charmingly excused himself and approached them. Thea looked up to view one of the most beautiful men she had ever seen.

"Peter, this is Althea Garrett." Jett said. "My Thea," he added.

"My Thea," Peter repeated as he looked into her eyes. Thea's knees got weak. Jett mumbled something about something in the oven and disappeared, much to Thea's dismay.

"How do you do?" Thea managed to murmur.

"Much better now." was his response. He was smiling, but he still hadn't taken his eyes from hers. He grabbed her hand and pulled her down the patio steps onto the lawn. They began walking toward the pool.

"Congratulations," she said breathlessly. "I know how much your family is looking forward to having you back on Nevis."

"Ah, yes. A double edged sword."

Thea said nothing, wishing she could have her family back, warts and all. Peter noticed her quiet, then it hit him. Jett had told him Thea's story. How callous of him. He stopped and grabbed her hand.

"I am so, so sorry. I..." he began. She realized Jett must have told him about her tragedies.

"It's OK. If you're talking about my losses, they're mine to deal with, and I shouldn't make others uncomfortable about it. I should be the one to apologize." She paused. "Just do yourself a favor? Love them. Unconditionally. It might hurt less when they go."

She moved away from him and continued to walk, hands clasped behind her back, head bowed.

"I feel like a fool," he said.

"Don't." she said. "Really. It's still a bit raw with me, that's all. People need to be able to joke and talk about their families' idiosyncrasies. I haven't met a family yet that doesn't have any." She was smiling. He exhaled.

"I understand your business is going quite well?" He tried to change the subject. The accent and the deep voice in combination gave her goosebumps.

"Yes, I've been quite busy. Would you like an official portrait for the Police Station?" she asked.

"Are you networking?" he kidded.

"All the time. A girl's gotta make a living."

"Would that portrait be in pastels or would it be a photograph?"

Jett had obviously told him quite a bit, and he had remembered.

"Your choice."

"Which one would require me to spend more time with you?" he asked, taking her hand again. She shyly looked up at him.

"Um, I usually work on pastel portraits from a photograph, so it's a wash."

"Too bad," he said as he pulled her closer. He was looking deeply into her eyes.

Just then Irene called Peter away, as an old friend had arrived to wish him well. He told Thea they would need to continue the conversation later. Thea was happy for the break in the intensity, and went back to her camera.

The meal was a feast like none the island had seen. Thea caught Peter looking her way all evening, and she realized she was watching him as well. When the crowd dispersed to the Great Room for coffee or onto the patio to hear the steel band, Peter found Thea and pulled her back out into the gardens. He found a secluded spot and took her hands.

"I know I'm being very forward," he said, "but I've been thinking about this all evening, and I want to kiss you." Before she could protest he had pulled her to him and had his mouth on hers. All the emotions she had bottled up in the last year came spilling out in that kiss. She had forgotten how it felt to be held and wanted. It was as if someone had opened her heart and let out some of the pain. Peter felt her trembling, yet she had put her arms around his waist and was returning his kiss, passionately no less. He held her face in his hands. When their lips parted he looked down at her, wanting to kiss her again. She stepped away from him and began to drift toward the patio. He reached out and took her hand.

"Don't go," he said. She turned toward him, still trembling. He could feel it.

"I'm not sure I trust myself to stay," she whispered, and then she turned and fled toward the Inn. Peter watched her graceful movements and felt the stirrings inside him. He would have to get close to her. He wanted her. But this night he had scared her away.

Peter was officially on holiday for another few days before returning to England to begin his relocation process. He thought about Thea most of the time, but whenever he called the Inn looking for her, she was out working. Jett reassured Peter that she was not avoiding him, but that she was busy with several weddings and a business convention at the island's big hotel.

Jett's night off was Friday. The Inn held a West Indian buffet, and Jett was able to prepare all the dishes ahead of time, and the other kitchen staff took over from there. It was his night to kick back with his friends, drink some beer and go to the Jump Up on the beach. He usually took Thea with him, as she loved the music, and loved to dance. His friends all adored Thea as well. They liked having and older woman around to ask advice of. She affectionately called them her posse. This night was no different. Jett called to her from the car park.

"T! You ready?"

She came down the stairs wearing white shorts, a black halter top and Teva sandals, and gold hoop earrings that flashed in the setting sunlight. She was tall, 5'9", her womanly body fit her height, and her long legs made her look taller than she was. Her Posse nicknamed her the big white woman in the most complimentary and affectionate sense. Thea and Jett took her Moke to the beach, and she dropped Jett by the band, as he carried a cooler of food for the festivities, and circled back to park. The posse saw Jett approaching.

"Where be the big white woman?"

"She be comin', mon." Jett fell into his patois easily with his buddies. Thea got kisses from all her boys when she showed up.

Lit torches lined the beach, and a fire was built. The band played a mix of old Reggae tunes and their own music, and the crowd was a mixture of locals with a few tourists thrown in. The locals sold beer out of big coolers for a buck, and as soon as everyone finished looking for the green flash as the sun dipped below the horizon, the dancing began. Thea was always pulled into the dancing early by one of her posse, and she never resisted, as it was almost a religious experience for her to dance barefoot in the sand with the breeze blowing her hair.

Peter arrived soon after the music began. His old friends and Jett's friends welcomed him, and someone handed him a beer. He stood at the back of the crowd, watching the dancers at the edge of the water. His 6'3" frame allowed him a clear view. Jett had told him that Thea usually came to the Jump Up, and he was looking for her in the crowd when he spotted her dancing with one of Jett's friends. Her fluid and sensual motion mesmerized him. The way her body swayed to the music aroused him, and when she turned he could see her eyes were half closed. She seemed to be in another place. He wondered if that was how she would look lying beneath him as he made love to her. She lifted her arms and swept her hair on top of her head as she turned. He could see her beautiful shoulders and her back bared by the halter-top. The sweat glistened on her skin. He became more turned on just watching her. The song ended and Thea stepped to the side to take a swig of her beer. Peter watched her run the cold bottle across her forehead, and he had to catch his breath when she used it to cool her neck and her cleavage. She was behind the crowd and no one seemed to be watching her, or so she thought. Peter put his empty bottle down and walked around the crowd to approach her from the back. She was messily piling her hair on top of her head and fastening it with a hair comb. The band was starting to play an old Gregory Issacs tune as Peter placed his palm on Thea's lower back and took her hand. Surprised, she looked up over her shoulder to see him. Her smile was welcoming, but he could see the apprehension in her eyes. He pulled her into the sea of slowly swaying dancers and held her close, wrapping her arms around his neck as he fanned his fingers over the base of her spine. He whispered to her.

"You've been avoiding me."

"No! Really, I haven't!"

"I'm not going to let you run away tonight."

Thea thought she'd swoon. He moved closer to her so he could whisper directly into her ear.

"I've been watching you dance. You look very far away when you dance, like you've been transported to another place. Where do you go, Thea?"

His voice was melting her. She loved hearing him say her name. She said nothing.

"I would like to take you to that place. I can, you know."

He was seducing her, and she was enjoying it. She kept telling herself it was OK, she wasn't being unfaithful to Kip. He was gone and it was all right for her to move on. She sighed.

"Will you let me, Thea? I'll make you feel so good. I want to bring you pleasure. Let me make love to you."

She was lost. He moved his mouth to hers and delicately kissed her, teasing her, licking and biting her lower lip. He had maneuvered them to the edge of the crowd, and now pulled her with him past the last of the torches on the beach. She ran with him to where the Nevis Hotel's beach cabanas stood, empty at this time of night. He pulled her to a secluded spot behind a stand of palms and took her into his arms. He tilted her head back and kissed her deeply, his tongue opening her lips, foretelling pleasures to come. He pulled her pelvis to his, and she could feel his hardness. He moved his hand to the side of her breast, and ran his thumb down the length of her ribcage. It was not an aggressive touch, but a tender stroke.

"May I touch you?" he whispered. He was being a gentleman and asking permission.

"Peter... I haven't done this in a really long time."

"Let me reacquaint you with the pleasures of lovemaking," he whispered as he licked at her earlobe, "I will be as gentle as you want me to be." He was giving her an opportunity to set the pace. "Thea, let me show you how good you can feel, I want to make love to you."

She moved her mouth to his and kissed him hungrily, taking his hand and moving it to her breast. He moaned as he felt her swollen nipple. He grabbed her hand and pulled her up the path.

"Where are we going?" she asked.

"This is where I am staying," he said. "I want you where I can have you all to myself, without interruption, and in comfort. Our first time together will not be a quickie on the beach."

He opened the door of his bungalow to reveal a turned down king-sized bed with a chalice vine flower on the pillow. His open suitcase was on the stand, and a small refrigerator stood next to the dresser. He closed the door and moved to put a lamp on.

"Don't ."

He looked at her and saw in the moonlight that she was nervous. He moved to her and kissed her.

"I want to see you," he whispered. He looked at her for a reply and she nodded. He put a low light on near the entrance to the bathroom. He moved back to her and removed his polo shirt. She ran her hands over his chest, enjoying the view. He reached for her waistband and unbuttoned her shorts. He slid the zipper down and ran his hands over her ass as he slid them off, watching her backside in the mirror. She wore a g-string. He exhaled audibly. He held the bottom of her halter and she lifted her arms so he could pull it off over her head. He reached behind and tugged gently at the hair comb, and her hair fell in red waves to her shoulders. He grabbed her hair in both hands and crushed her face to his in a deep kiss, moaning as she rubbed her pelvis against the front of his pants. He finished undressing, and reached for the waist of her g-string, pulling it off with two fingers. He looked at her with longing, studying her breasts and her belly, and the red curls beneath. He sat on the edge of the bed and pulled her toward him. She stood between his legs and held his shoulders as he took her nipple in his mouth. He bit gently, licking it as he held it between his teeth, sending an exquisite chill down her spine. His hands rubbed her bottom, squeezing and kneading her flesh. Her head fell back as she sighed. He rose and guided her to the bed. As she lay back on the white sheets he took the chalice flower and placed it between her breasts, kissing each one in turn. She would never be able to experience that scent again without thinking of that moment. He rose and kissed her.

"Lay back and let me make you come."

She ached with longing. He moved down and opened her legs to his tongue. He licked and bit that precious orb of pleasure, sucking her wetness and making her writhe. As she would approach her climax he would back off and not allow her to reach it, until she begged him not to stop. When she came he lifted his eyes to watch her, and saw the expression of mingled pleasure and pain on her beautiful face. He watched her back arch and her fingers splayed and then clutching the bedclothes. He thought he could come just watching her. He wanted to keep her pleasure from stopping and rose to enter her. He feared hurting her and took her palm in his hand and kissed it, moving it to his manhood. She opened her eyes in surprise when she touched him.

"Oh, God!" she said. He smiled at her. "I don't want to hurt you," he whispered. "Guide me."

She rose on her elbow and kissed him. She could taste her sweetness on his lips and it excited her even more. She lifted her hips and brought his member to her, easing him into her slowly, the exquisite pain not more than the pleasure, gasping, until he was as far as she could take him. He remained still for a moment, looking down upon her half-closed eyes. He waited for her motion to cue him, and she moved her hips slowly. He began to gently fuck her, her moans a signal he should not stop. Before long her rapid breath foretold of her coming. She looked up at him, almost embarrassed at her abandon.

"You are so beautiful. I want to watch you come again."

Her eyes closed as her head fell back and he watched, and was once again enchanted by the release. He continued to move with her and rubbed her nipples as her pleasure mounted once more. She came several more times before he could stand it no longer. He had been close to climax for too long and couldn't hold himself back.

"Oh, Thea." was his moan as his release overtook him. She looked up to see the tension in his face smooth to calm as he thrust one last time into her. He bent his head and kissed her deeply, moving his arm around her and pulling her onto her side as he lay down on the bed. He held her close as he panted, and said nothing until his breathing steadied.

"How are you?" he asked.

"Sated. Exhausted. Grateful."

"Grateful?" he rose up onto his elbow and looked at her.

"That wasn't an insult! I haven't been with a man in over a year and a half. It could have been awkward or worse... horrible. You were so," she paused, "generous." She whispered haltingly. "You made me feel beautiful and special. And you're an incredible lover. So, yes, I'm grateful."

He watched her as she spoke. It was obvious that she was searching for the right words. He leaned toward her and kissed her again.

"You are beautiful and special. I know this happened quickly, but I feel like I've known you forever. Jett speaks of you all the time."

"I feel the same way, should we thank him?" she asked.

"Not a chance. Brothers don't let on that they're appreciative of each other. It's a sign of weakness."

"One thing I never asked Jett, and after being with you I have to," she began. He looked on earnestly. "You're so handsome, and charming, and good in bed, how is it that you're not married?"

He rolled his eyes and laughed out loud.

"That wasn't what I was expecting. I *was* married, briefly. I met a beautiful Jamaican woman in England when we were both is school. We dated for a while, sort of off and on, and after university she went back to Jamaica. I became a barrister, and she went to work for her family's manufacturing business. She came to England and materialized at my flat one day, saying how she'd missed me and could we perhaps get back together. She, well, moved in, and we lived together for a while. It was OK, I dunno, I wasn't in love with her, but I'm not sure I know what love is, really. The natural progression was to marry. She didn't want a big event, so a friend of mine married us in a small private ceremony. Our families were... shocked I guess is the right word. They supported the marriage, though, and we were all right for a bit. The problem started when I became a copper. All of a sudden the hours were different and it was dangerous. I guess she got lonely. We tried to work it out, we talked about kids, but she was afraid I'd be killed and she'd have to raise them on her own. We continued to drift apart, and then she told me she was seeing someone else. She wanted a divorce, and I didn't have enough feeling for her to want to try anymore, so I gave her one. We were married for 3 years. It seems a very long time ago. Being a cop in London is very tough on a relationship. I've never gotten serious with anyone since."

Thea just looked at his profile.

"It's hard to believe she stepped out on you."

"Why?"

"I've sampled the merchandise."

She watched his mouth curve into a smile. He rolled over and on top of her, pushing her down on the sheets. As he kissed her she could feel the stirring in his loins.

"I want to fuck you again," he whispered, sliding his tongue into her mouth before she could agree or object, and moving his cock into her heat. He pushed slowly, teasingly. She lifted her hips to meet him, and worked herself on him with abandon. He rolled over, pulling her on top of him, and she rode him like a wild stallion, leaning back to hold his legs as he worked her hips. Her climax was fast and violent, and noisy. He was so turned on by her sounds and actions that he came almost immediately after her, and she fell onto him and kissed and bit him as he moaned with pleasure.

They eventually rose and dressed, and went back to the beach. Thea knew Jett would worry if she just disappeared all night. Even Peter didn't want to cause his brother that much angst. The party was going strong when they returned, but Jett had noticed them missing. Both of them. When they returned he gave them a knowing and disapproving look. He approached them and kissed Thea on the cheek and whispered to her, "Watch out for him, he's a rogue and a scoundrel." Peter smiled contentedly. "I know," she replied to Jett. Peter looked like he'd just been slapped.

Thea asked Jett if he had a ride home, and he nodded. She took Peter's hand and led him to the Moke.

"Take me back to your room. I feel like a woman who's been deprived of oxygen for 18 months and now I can't breathe enough."

The look on his face was pure lust. He pulled her to him, slid his tongue between her lips and rubbed her thighs. She rubbed his pelvis with hers suggestively. He took her keys, drove her to his hotel and made love to her all night.

Peter went and returned from England and was installed as Chief of Police on Nevis. He and Thea spent their free time together. She cooked dinners at his house, he visited the Inn to see her studio and posed for his portrait, and they spent lust filled nights exploring each other's bodies. Thea never did anything to insinuate herself into his world. She never left anything at his house, was never possessive, and never attempted to take the relationship any further. They liked each other, but she disagreed with some of his politics, and they found they didn't have a whole lot in common other than sex. One night after making love, Peter reached for her and held her, stroking her hair and studying her face. "What?" she asked.

"I can't decipher you. You float in and out of my day, and make me happy and crazy and yet you demand nothing of me."

"Like what?" she looked confused.

"A shelf in my armoire. Marriage. Children." he replied.

Her look turned serious.

"Peter, how old do you think I am?"

It was his turn to look confused.

"You're my age, what? 35?" he said. He'd never asked and she'd never told.

"That's very flattering, but I'll be 41 this year. I had my tubes tied when I was 38. I can't have children."

Peter looked as if he'd been struck. His face softened.

"We could adopt."

"I don't want kids! I never have!" she said, head shaking in disbelief. "Peter you aren't in love with me. You're in lust. Besides, your father wants you to marry a nice island girl and have all those babies."

"He said that?"

"No. I just know. He's from an older generation. He wants his island to remain of his people, and I can't blame him. That's one of the reasons he was so happy to have you back. You can continue the name, you and eventually Jett. I'd spent some time with your father before I met you, he was pretty forthcoming about his heritage and his beliefs."

"I have a say in this, you know!" he said laughingly, eyes wide.

"Yeah, you do. And you just said you wanted to get married and have babies. That's not going to happen with me."

"Aren't you in love with me?" he asked, brows furrowed. She hesitated.

"I love you, Peter. But no, I'm not in love with you."

"How can you tell?" He looked hurt, but his question seemed sincere. She took a while to answer.

"Because I feel like I could go on without you." She continued. "You know, I'm not sure I know what being in love feels like."

"Weren't you in love with Kip?"

"I don't know. We were good together, we had a good life. I might have just blocked it out, but I don't think so."

"Do you think you're not letting yourself be in love with me?" He'd rolled onto his back.

She considered his remark.

"You know, I've thought about that. It's easy to say 'I've been hurt, and I won't let myself fall in love' but I don't think if it happened and I was faced with it that I'd be able to override the emotion. So, no, I don't think that's it. Please don't be hurt! I can't tell you how wonderful this relationship has been for me. You're responsible for a lot of my healing, and I'll always love you and be thankful to you for that. You let me feel again. I wasn't sure I could for a while. But I don't know if this island is forever for me! I think its part of my healing, too. Someday I'm probably going to discover that it's OK to go back to Boston, or somewhere, and stop hiding. I realize now that hiding is what I'm doing here."

"What do you mean?"

"I have total control over my world here. It's small, not overwhelming, it surrounds me in beauty. People are happy here, because they're on vacation. Life is slow. It's so opposite from the reality I'm used to. I've blocked out that reality, the same as if I'd hidden in a closet. When, and if, I feel healthy enough to face it I'll probably go back, and come out of hiding. But for right now this is what I want." She studied his face. "You know, Peter, maybe we should..." She paused. He was staring at the ceiling. "Maybe I should give you the chance to find the woman to have those babies with."

"What do you mean?" His voice was flat.

"If we don't see each other you can start seeing other woman."

"My options on this island are limited." He couldn't believe they were having this conversation.

"I bet you haven't even looked on St. Kitts." She was smiling and trying to be lighthearted for him, but the thought of leaving was tearing her up. She'd miss how safe she felt in his arms, how well loved.

"That's it then? You leave and I start trying to find a wife?" he said sarcastically.

"Don't settle, Peter. You deserve to have everything you want. Everything." She kissed him gently, rolled out of bed, slipped on her clothes and quietly left. It was easy to leave, physically, as she had nothing there to take with her. It was as though she knew all along that this is how it would be. She got into the mini Moke and as she pulled out into the road she began to cry.

There was more gossip about Peter and Thea parting than there had been about their relationship. Jett was distraught by it, and only Irene knew the whole story. Peter, ever the gentleman, never spoke about Thea except in kind and loving terms, and after several months apart they were able to see each other in social situations easily, without the tension they felt after first breaking up. Thea stopped going to Jump Ups for awhile, afraid she'd see him and be tempted. Peter missed her, and many times wanted to go to her and tell her he wouldn't be settling if he chose her. But he understood that the island would not always be home to her, and after many years away from it he had returned for good. Peter made attempts to see other women. He had a cousin on St. Kitts who introduced him to people there, but his heart really wasn't in it. He was busy with his office, and he was involved in a multi Caribbean Island anti-drug initiative that took up a lot of his time. One night after a dinner meeting held at the Figtree Inn,

Peter ran into Thea as he went to speak with his brother in the kitchen. Jett was nowhere to be found and Thea was taking the last bite of a salad she was eating while standing in the doorway looking out at the blue water of the illuminated swimming pool. There she was, with her beautiful back and shoulders exposed by one of those bloody sundresses. He trampled over his willpower on the way to the door, slipped his arms around her and tenderly kissed her shoulder. Her head snapped around to see who was holding her. She smiled sadly and shook her head.

"Peter, what are you doing?" she whispered.

"I thought it was obvious," he replied, grinning.

"This isn't good!" she admonished, "It's hard enough seeing you around without this!"

"So, you've missed me, too?"

"Of course I have. Did you think I wouldn't?"

"Did you miss me, or did you miss me fucking you?" he said in her ear. She hung her head. He knew the answer, and he would settle for that if he had to.

"How about sex with no ties?" he asked. "Not all the time. Just when one of us... needs..."

"You're serious?" she asked. He hadn't removed his arms from her waist, and was still kissing her shoulder.

"No ties. No responsibility. I won't ask anything of you. We'll just occasionally make each other feel good. How 'bout it?" he asked.

And so Thea and Peter began the second phase of their relationship, which consisted of sex to scratch an itch. They both realized it would be very easy to fall back into their old ways, so they never told a soul and limited their clandestine meetings to once in a great while when neither of them could stand it anymore.

The night Peter responded to Jett's call made the first time in several months that he'd seen Thea. He'd been thinking about her and knew he'd need to find her soon. As soon as Peter headed up the stairs to her room, the ever hopeful Jett had put a chain across the stairs with an "employees only" sign on it so they wouldn't be disturbed.

THREE

Jasper Collins stood on the forward observation deck of The Victoria and looked at the lights of Charlestown. His mind raced with the thoughts of all that had happened. The problems facing him were not bad enough that he had the additional guilt of leaving that woman on the beach. She'd helped him, and quite possibly saved his life. His entire midsection hurt from the blows he'd received, but there weren't any other complications.

He wasn't letting Charles talk him into going to hospital, but he did agree to let a local doctor see him, on board, after several hours of arguing. The doctor said there would be bruising, and to rest. Brilliant. He told the doctor it was from a fall, and asked if he'd seen anyone else that evening. He was trying to determine if he'd done the tosser that hit him enough damage to seek treatment, or if, God help him, they had come back and hurt that woman. The doctor complained that the only disturbance to his evening was being dragged by launch to this yacht in the harbor. Charles paid the doctor in cash, and Tim and Roy motored him back to the pier. Charles found Jas and poured him a drink.

"You know, this was an attempt on your life and should be reported," he said to the younger man as he handed him the cognac.

"I think it was a warning." Jas continued to stare at the Nevis capital. "Just think what the press would do with that information. It's just what they want."

"Sir, do you really think this is related to the purchase? What if it's another matter altogether?" Charles asked. Jas Collins was attempting to purchase a grocery chain in the US whose union employees were viewing his above board purchase offer as a union busting takeover.

"Please, Charles. What else?" It was more a statement than a question. "My daughter is threatening to run off with a heavy metal band, one of our affiliates has just reported a futures purchasing error to the tune of $6.8 million and my sister is getting married on this blasted island in three days to a man whose been wed 3 times. Which of those others might it be related to? The heavy metal band?"

Charles said nothing. Jas laughed sadly, and then held his stomach in pain.

"Where is Victoria?" he asked.

"She's below in her stateroom, sir. Shall I call for her?"

"No. I'm sure she's still spitting after the row we had earlier. I don't need any more excitement just now. You needn't stay here, Charles. Go enjoy what's left of the evening."

"Very good, sir." Charles left him alone.

Jas could see Tim, Roy and Duncan patrolling the deck. It was a horrible world when men of standing were faced with kidnapping and death threats and had to employ bodyguards to keep their families safe. He was still annoyed with Duncan for disobeying his order to go back and help the woman on the beach. He knew their allegiance was to him, and their training forced them to see all others as a threat, even that helpful woman. He couldn't help but smile when he thought of her dropping that gorilla to his knees. What had she done, kicked him? It all happened behind him, and so fast. He knew he was a fool to go for a run by himself like that. After his row with Victoria she had threatened to strike out on her own on the island and he ordered the men to take her back to the yacht. He'd stayed on shore so she would stop screaming, since her assault was aimed at him. He was so distraught. It seemed his whole world was one big problem just then. He'd experienced hostile acquisitions before, the futures mistake would hurt but certainly not break the corporation. And his sister had to be responsible for her own life. Thankfully her fiancé had signed the pre-nuptial agreement (after Jas had offered a rather large wedding gift in return). But matters regarding Victoria always did him in. How could a girl whom he'd raised for 16 years suddenly become such a stranger to him? Exercise had always helped him clear his head, so he began to jog down the beach. The hard sand felt good under his feet, and the color of the water reflecting the low hanging sun soothed him. He covered a fair distance quickly, and realized the cove would block his view of the yacht, so he stopped. His crew would be frantic if they couldn't see him. He looked up to see the launch headed toward him when the two men attacked him.

Jas' stomach tightened when he thought of it, sending a spasm through his ribs. His crew would have to be on the alert, as Victoria might be in danger as well.

FOUR

Dick Corcoran had been the head of the union controlling the World Markets warehouse for 17 years. He'd been well taken care of by members and union bosses alike, as he'd always been able to fend off possible warehouse closings because of the dirt that he'd dug up on the members of the World Markets board. But now Ted Sablan, the man on which he had the most dirt had gone and gotten himself killed in a boating accident, and the rest of the board members were voting to sell, which meant closing the warehouse for sure. All of Corcoran's people would be out of work, and he'd be lucky to make it out alive. That realization was the beginning of his uneasy alliance with Victor Sablan, the biggest remaining shareholder, to whom his deceased brother had bequeathed his shares. If the late brother's tastes tended toward the seedy, then perhaps Victor had unusual tastes as well. Corcoran knew he'd have to dig fast, and in the meantime try to work a deal with Sablan in case he unearthed nothing useful. Sablan had agreed to a meeting, thinking it was to allay the union's fears about their future now that his brother was gone. The two men met in Sablan's office and exchanged pleasantries.

"Dick, what can I do for you?" Victor Sablan began.

"Victor, you've known me for a long time, and you know I don't mince words. I understand the board has decided to sell?" he replied.

"We've received an offer, but no decision has been made at this time," he hedged.

"You know," Corcoran began, "if the company looking at us has half a brain they'll question the cost of doing business from the logistics end."

"Why is that?" Sablan asked coolly.

"Because the costs are too low. Your brother knew what the real costs of running the warehouse operations were, but was protecting us from a possible closure and move to a wholesaler."

"Why would he cook the books if it wasn't good for the company?" Sablan asked innocently. He suspected as much all along, but this man could give him the skinny.

"Shall we say he had 'an arrangement' with the union?" Corcoran said, rubbing his chin. It wasn't true, but Sablan probably didn't know it.

"I'll need to look into this. If the business plan is not correct, then we'll have to make the appropriate changes."

Corcoran cut him off. "That might not be the best idea. You don't want that kind of information becoming public knowledge, do you? That your brother was in bed with the union? There might be other things that could come out."

Sablan's face didn't change, but his insides were in turmoil. He knew of his brother's tastes in kinky sex and surmised that this bastard had some additional information of which Victor wasn't even aware.

"What would you suggest?" he asked.

"I've actually already put a plan into motion. We've, shall we say, sent a message to the potential buyer that perhaps this isn't a company he's really interested in. I'm sure you'll be hearing from him."

"You threatened Jasper Collins?" Sablan was incredulous. He knew Collins not to be a man who backed down easily.

"We just sent him a message. That's all. And I would suggest you pull the deal off the table." Corcoran added.

"What if I can't?" Sablan was getting nervous, wondering if the next message sent would be to him.

"Then perhaps we need to negotiate my settlement if the deal does happen to go through." Corcoran figured if he worked both ends that he might end up both alive and wealthy.

That began the uneasy alliance of Dick Corcoran and Victor Sablan. Sablan worked up a payoff that would appease Corcoran, keep Sablan's family name untarnished and keep he and his family from bodily harm, and Corcoran began searching for Victor's skeletons to make himself richer. If the deal went through then Corcoran would just have to quickly disappear. If it didn't, he'd hopefully have enough on Victor Sablan to keep the warehouse functioning and his graft coming in until his retirement. Life was good again.

FIVE

At first light Thea kicked Peter out of bed and told him to get home before the whole island knew they'd spent the night together. They'd been careful before, leaving at a reasonable hour so no one's suspicions would be raised. Last night Thea was needy, and Peter was more than happy to oblige. They didn't sleep until almost 3 AM, he was too exhausted to move, or she to kick him out, so he stayed, happily wound in her arms.

As he fumbled down the stairs he almost tripped on the chain at the bottom, and mumbled to no one in particular "Somebody knows."

Peter went home, slept for another two hours, showered, dressed and went into the station, expecting perhaps some news related to Thea's story. He had his dispatcher put in calls to a few people for him. He wasn't disappointed. The phone rang at 10 AM and his dispatcher called into him.

"Chief, Dr. White is on the phone." Peter answered the call.

"Chief Moses here."

"Peter? Angus White."

"Good morning Dr. White. How are you?"

"I'm well, Peter. How is your father?"

"Fine, sir, just fine."

"What can I do for you this day?"

"Doctor, did you treat anyone last night with injuries that might have been received in a fight?"

"Peter, I'm not supposed to discuss such things, you know that."

"Yes, but there may have been a commission of a crime."

"Well, something strange occurred last evening. I was summoned out to a yacht in the harbor to examine a man who injured his abdomen in a fall, or so he said."

"You didn't believe him?" Peter was chuckling to himself.

"I've seen enough in my day to know blows from a punch when I see them." The doctor seemed impatient.

"I don't doubt you, sir. I have some other information that corroborates your theory. Can you come in and look at some photographs for me?" Peter asked.

"Yes, but why? I can't tell you who the man is."

"If his yacht is in the harbor then I can tell you he's Jasper Collins, the corporate tycoon from the U.K." Peter responded.

"Ah, you were always very bright."

"Will you come in? I'd like to know if you recognize some other people as well."

"What time?"

"About one?" Peter asked.

"Certainly. All the best for the day, Peter." The doctor rang off. Peter picked up the phone and dialed the Inn. Irene answered.

"Irene, its Peter Moses. May I please speak with Thea?"

Irene put down the phone and went though the kitchen and yelled up the back stair for Thea. Jett heard her tell Thea who it was and picked up the phone himself.

"What time did you leave this morning, Romeo?" Jett asked his brother before even saying hello.

"None of your business you little wanker." Peter was smiling when he said it, now knowing it was Jett who put the chain across Thea's steps. "And it's no one

51

else's business, either, do you understand?" He heard Jett laugh and then Thea was on the phone.

"Hi, what was that all about?"

"Brotherly love. I found out who the bloody bastard is who left you on the beach last night."

"Really? Who? How?" Thea was jolted awake by the information from her groggy state after only a few hours of sleep.

"Jasper Collins." Peter answered. "I spoke to the Harbor Master first thing this morning. The launch was his. Can you have the photographs here by one?"

"Sure. Do you mean the guy who's taking over the World Markets grocery chain in the US?" she asked.

"Do you know him?" Peter was surprised.

"I do have a phone line for Internet access. I haven't totally lost touch with the world, you know."

"I have his dossier in front of me. It pays to keep friends in British Intelligence. One o'clock, then." He lowered his voice. "You were wild last night, woman."

"Take a cold shower, Spanky. I'll see you at one." Thea heard Peter laughing as she hung up.

SIX

Thea made enlargements of all of the facial shots and pertinent photos from her roll of film. She drove to the Police Station at 12:45 and found Peter in his office. They spread the photos out on the desk, and shortly after, the doctor entered. He pointed out the launch in which he'd been transported to the yacht. He alluded to the fact that he'd seen the blond man on the yacht, although he was hesitant to speak about his treatment of the man. He did not know the two men on the beach. He'd treated no one else last night at Alexandra Hospital, but he'd called the hospital on St. Kitts this morning after speaking to Peter, and they might have treated the men.

Peter faxed the photographs of the men to Joseph N. France General Hospital and followed up with a phone call. Yes, the two men had been there. One had been treated and released for a broken jaw, the other wasn't treated, but had obvious lower back distress, both claiming they had fought each other. They paid in cash, which was quite odd, and no address was given. Peter sat rubbing his chin, looking out the window.

"What now?" Thea asked.

"I'm going to scan their photos into the computer and e-mail them to the authorities in the US and England. They could still be here, and they could still be a threat to Collins and to you." Peter looked at her with concern. Thea put her hands up.

"Hey, I'll lay low! I promise."

"Do you have jobs this week?" he asked.

"Just one on Saturday. A wedding in the afternoon."

"Either one of the officers or I will be with you."

"Peter! How comfortable is THAT going to make the bride and groom?" she said, voice rising. "They NEVER SAW ME."

"Woman, there will be no discussion." he said quietly. "I will be there, and I will be in plain clothes. OK?"

Thea rolled her eyes.

"Yes, Mon Capitan!" she said with a mock salute. As she left his office she heard the sound of the scanner and a modem engaging.

SEVEN

Sal Salvetti and Joey Landolfi slept late at the seedy hotel by the St. Kitts airport. Sal's broken jaw hurt like crazy and he mumbled even worse now when he talked. Joey was afraid every time he took a piss he was going to see blood. He was sure his kidneys had failed after that bitch kicked him, it hurt so friggin' bad. Joey wasn't looking forward to calling the boss and telling him they hadn't delivered the message as completely as instructed. When they were both awake enough and Sal was able to take in a little coffee through a straw, they called in.

"Yeah, Boss. It's Joey. Where's Sal? Uh, he's indisposed. No, he's not in the can. He, uh, well, we ran into a little trouble last night. No, we're not in jail. He got his jaw busted by the target. I know, I know. It was bad enough we couldn't get him alone, when we finally did his boys came pretty quick and, um, another party, a fucking good Samaritan helped him out. No we didn't hurt her. Yeah it was a broad. I know, I know. Sal landed a couple to his gut, but we didn't have time to do more. Watta ya want us to do? Go back after him again? Ok, yeah. Ok, we'll find out where he's goin'. Don't touch him, just keep an eye on him? Ok, we'll call in a couple of days." Joey hung up the phone. "The boss wants us to hire a boat and keep an eye on Collins. He gave me a name of one of them runners we use when we bring the stuff in from South America. We gotta call in a couple of days for more instructions. Capisce?"

Sal just mumbled.

EIGHT

Peter had the Harbor Master motor him out to the Victoria. The crew checked his credentials and he was announced on board. An older gentleman in a suit approached him.

"Good day, Sir. May I help you?"

"I hope so. I am Chief Peter Moses of the Nevis Police Department. I would like to speak with Mr. Jasper Collins."

"I am Charles Marston, Mr. Collins' secretary. May I be of any assistance?"

Before Peter could answer Jasper Collins entered the main salon from the steps leading to the sundeck. He was dressed in dark pants and a buttoned down shirt with the cuffs rolled up.

"It's alright, Charles. I'll speak with Chief Moses. Won't you join me?" Peter followed Jasper Collins into the fantail salon where he motioned for Peter to sit. "Coffee? Or something cold?"

"No, thank you." Peter noticed a young woman in a bright orange tie died swimsuit, with a Walkman, sitting on a deck chair in the sun. He turned back to Collins who was carrying a coffee mug.

"Mr. Collins, I won't mince words. You were attacked last night on the northwestern end of Pinney's Beach by two men, and I'd like to know why you chose not to report it."

Jas' face did not change. He looked down at the carpet, thought for a moment, looked at Peter and said "If a personal injury is not reported and the injured party chooses not to press charges, has a crime been committed? Besides, how do you know this happened?"

Peter pulled the photographs out the folder and spread them out on the table in front of them. Jasper's face was still unchanged, except for a slight narrowing of his eyes. Peter spoke.

"To answer your question, it is still a crime. Assault is assault. I did not come out here because a crime was committed necessarily; I came because the two men who attacked you are members of a rogue organized crime operation. Their specialty is, shall we say, sending messages. Abducting children, breaking the legs of those who do not do as they are told, and other such things. They probably would not have killed you, but we don't know what the people who paid for their services requested. They were in St. Kitts last night. But we don't know where they are now."

"You still have not answered my question. There are no actual pictures of the attack, unless the photographer saved them for the tabloids. How do you know it happened?" Jasper Collins said quietly. Peter became annoyed.

"Because you broke the jaw of one of your assailants. Because the woman you deserted on the beach last night to fend for herself told me. Who do you think took the bloody pictures?"

Jas closed his eyes and exhaled. It was the first emotion Peter had seen from the man.

"Is she alright?" he asked.

"Yes."

"Thank God." Jasper Collins sat back and looked as if a weight had been lifted from his shoulders. "Please believe me when I tell you I have thought of nothing else since the incident happened. My bodyguards are trained to remove me from the threat. I sent them back to look for her but she was gone."

Peter wasn't sure why, but he believed him.

"She brought that bloody gorilla to his knees! I worried that they might have found her. Will she be safe from them?"

"I have seen to her safety myself, Mr. Collins."

"Please, call me Jas."

"Then call me Peter. Jas, I'm concerned about you, and your daughter. I have limited resources here and can only afford you so much protection. I know you have your own guards. Are they armed?"

"Not always, but they will be from now on."

"You might be safer in England."

"Peter, I don't disagree, but my sister is to be married here this weekend. I cannot return until early next week."

Ah, Peter thought, Thea's Saturday job.

"Then let me offer whatever assistance I might give until then." He handed Jas his card. "Please let me know when you are coming ashore so I may offer you additional protection."

"Thank you. Would you do me the favor of thanking the woman who came to my assistance last night? I owe her a great deal."

"I'll do that."

Peter did not offer that she would probably be photographing Jas' sister's wedding on Saturday and he could thank her himself. The fewer people who knew of her involvement the safer she would be.

Peter left by the deck ladder, passing the orange suited young woman.

"Are you really a cop or is that a good humor uniform?" she asked sarcastically.

He turned and looked at her. "The punishment for disrespecting a law enforcement officer in Nevis is to cut you up and use you for shark bait. Be careful."

Peter made eye contact with Jas as the girl made a face. He waved to Peter as the Harbor Master pulled away.

NINE

Peter's officers checked all incoming passengers at the ferry dock and the airport against the photographs Thea had taken of the men. They seemingly had not returned by conventional means, but Peter posted an officer at the Figtree Inn that night anyway. He knew he'd be pushing his luck to try to bed Thea two nights in a row, even with the excuse that it was for her own protection. He hadn't spoken to her since he paid his call to Jasper Collins.

Friday was relatively uneventful as well, until Peter received a call from the ship to shore operator late in the afternoon. It was Jas Collins calling for Peter Moses.

"Jas, how can I help?"

"I have a favor to ask. My daughter Victoria is insisting on coming to shore for the Jump Up. Should I be concerned? I was planning to send two of my men with her. I wanted your opinion."

"We aim to please our tourists! There is always an officer in uniform in attendance, and several of my men go to party with their families. I'm usually there myself, but I have a meeting tonight. I'll ask them to look out for her. I think she will be quite safe."

"Peter, thank you. It's difficult with a teenager, you promise them a holiday and end up holding them captive."

"I can quite imagine."

Jas rang off, and Peter wondered what life was like for the daughter of a multimillionaire. Things could be worse, he thought.

Thea brought her camera to the Jump Up that night. She was working on a new brochure for the Figtree Inn, and wanted to use some candid shots of

Island life. She used some super fast film so she wouldn't have to use a flash, and augmented the fading light with the beach torches. Jett's friends helped her move some of them around and were happily photographed dancing in the sand. Thea had not noticed the entourage make its way to the beach, and when she ended her impromptu photo shoot she realized she was being studied by a teenage girl in cutoff jeans and a black Soundgarden tee shirt. The girl had a few more ear piercings than necessary, but thankfully hadn't taken a needle or ink to any other body parts that were visible. She was almost as tall as Thea, with sandy colored long hair, parted in the middle. All Thea could think of was how she probably looked exactly like that at her age, but with red hair, and her shirt would have said The Moody Blues. The girl was quite pretty, but had overdone the eyeliner, which seemed to be a fashion statement these days. Thea had swigged a couple of beers already and was feeling somewhat playful, so she approached the young woman with her camera. She was smiling as she snapped a couple of torch lit close-ups, and when the band stopped she started singing, "Follow me into the dessert as thirsty as you are".

The girl looked stunned. "You know that song?"

"Yeah, I love Soundgarden. That bass player just does me in, babe."

The girl laughed. Her protectors moved in when Thea walked in front of her for another shot and they saw the camera. She suddenly had a big guy at each elbow.

"Oh, Hell-o." Thea recognized them from the beach on Wednesday night. "Fancy meeting you here!"

"Miss, we can't allow you to take pictures of the young lady." Thea detected a cockney lilt. She realized then that the teenager was Victoria Collins, daughter of

Jasper, whom she'd been researching on the Internet earlier that day.

"Does the young lady have a say?" Thea asked. "Or do you always bulldoze your employers around like you did on the beach two nights ago?" Thea realized then that she'd had too much beer.

"What? What happened two nights ago?" Victoria asked. The bodyguards were looking wide-eyed at Thea and trying to signal her to shut up. It was too late.

"Your father was attacked on the beach, didn't he tell you?" Thea said. Victoria's mouth fell open.

"Oh, bloody hell." Thea heard one of them mutter. "And how would you know that, Miss?" he said a little louder.

"Because I'm the one you left in the sand, asshole. Did you ever stop to think that those two morons might have come back for me?" Thea hadn't realized how angry she was about being left there till just then. Victoria looked at Roy, one of her protectors, for an answer.

"We're really sorry about that, Miss. Our first priority is always to get Mr. Collins to safety. He didn't want to leave you there. We got a right dressing down, we did, 'cause we wouldn't turn back for ya."

At that point Duncan chimed in. "We went back after Mr. Collins was safe on the yacht, Roy and I did. You were already gone." Victoria looked as if she would either cry or scream.

"Why didn't anybody tell me?" she asked.

"He didn't want to worry you, Miss." Duncan replied. Thea calmed down a bit.

"Is he alright? He took a couple of good ones to the gut," she asked.

"He was hurt?" Now Victoria looked like she really was going to cry.

"He's fine. We brought a doctor out to look at him. He's sore is all. He was more worried about what might have happened to you. I think he'll be relieved to hear we saw you and you're fine. By the way, nice side kick. Where'd you learn that?"

"You saved my father?" Victoria looked like she was about to implode.

"No, your boys here showed up just in time. I merely diminished the extent of his injuries." She turned to Duncan. "Tae Bo classes and kick boxing. I had never used it in anger, and hope never to do so again."

"You nailed him!" Duncan was laughing. Thea noticed that Victoria was still looking distressed. She grabbed the girl's elbow and pulled her down the beach a bit.

"Gentlemen, Miss Collins and I were talking before you interrupted us. I'm confident you'll remain a discreet distance while we continue?" She winked at Duncan, who smiled at her. The big boys kept watch but gave the ladies some privacy as they walked down the beach a little further and sat in the sand.

"Have you done any modeling?" Thea asked her.

"What? No!"

"You could, you know. You're lovely, Victoria. Do people call you Victoria?"

"Slow down! How do you know who I am? And how do you know my father?" The girl's mind was whirling. "And who are you?"

Thea laughed.

"I'm sorry. My name is Althea Garrett, my friends call me Thea, or on this island where they sometimes forget the H they call me T." She smiled, and the teenager seemed to be calming down a bit. "I don't know you, or your father. I'm a photographer here and I just happened to be on the far end of the beach when your father was attacked. I got some pictures of the guys who did it, and of your dad. I took them to the police. They told me who your father was. I used to be in the food business, and I knew the name, so I looked him up on the Internet. The story I read said he'd named his yacht after his only child. It wouldn't take a rocket scientist to figure out that you are Victoria." Thea paused to let it all sink in.

"What do your friends call you? Vicky?"

"No. Tori."

"Ah, like Tori Amos?"

"What are you li-ike." The girl said laughingly. Thea smiled.

"Not bad for an old broad, huh?"

"How old *are* you?" Tori asked.

"You know, you're never supposed to ask a woman that question." Thea chided. "I'm 39, and have been for 2 years." They both laughed out loud.

"What other bands do you like?" Tori asked.

"My current favorite is The Low Fidelity All-Stars."

"I love them! Do you like the Chemical Brothers?"

"Oh, yeah. Their newest CD is a lot like the music I was listening to in 1972. You should let your dad listen to it."

Tori made a face. She shook her head.

"What?" Thea asked.

"He doesn't get it. He just, oh, I don't know. We can't communicate."

"Do you try?" Thea asked. Tori shrugged.

"See, he didn't even tell me he'd been attacked."

"Really, Tori. What was he going to say? Some guys beat me up a little while ago on the beach sweetie, how was *your* night?" Thea paused. "Don't you have anything in common? Did you ever?"

"It's almost like he's afraid of me now. Now that I'm…" she paused.

"A woman? Who has breasts and periods?" Thea asked.

"Uh huh." Tori looked like she would cry.

"You know, your hormones are raging right now, too. Don't you have a woman you can talk to?"

"My mother took off when I was a baby. I don't even remember her. My silly aunt is such a floozy! And my dad just doesn't get it!" Tears rolled down the girl's cheeks. "He hasn't hugged me in forever. Every time we talk we end up screaming at each other."

Thea moved closer to the girl and put her arm around her. Tori clung to her and sobbed.

"You know, your father is probably just as upset about your relationship as you are. I bet if you just sat and told him how you felt…"

The girl wiped her eyes and looked at Thea.

"I just miss having a mother, not that I even know what that is like…"

"Your father never remarried?"

"No. He has women he sees once in awhile, but he's never even talked about it. Besides, they've never been interested in me. And they're not cool. Not like you!"

Thea laughed. "You've known me for half an hour and already I'm cool?"

Tori sniffed, and laughed, too. "Thanks for letting me talk."

"I think it's your father you need to talk to."

They sat and discussed womanly things. Thea told her about evening primrose and uva ursi for when she had PMS, and told her how exercise would make her feel better. Tori had all sorts of questions about the facts of life. They bonded. Tori was happy she'd found a new friend. They promised to e-mail each other after Tori's holiday.

"How long are you staying?" Thea asked.

"I think we're leaving early. I heard my father and that old fart Charles discussing it. We at least have to stay for the wedding."

"Who's wedding?"

"My aunt, the floozy. It's tomorrow."

"At the Island Garden?" Thea asked. Tori nodded.

"Guess what? I'm the photographer!"

Tori let out a shriek of delight and hugged her. The bodyguards had been watching them with great interest.

"Are you a bridesmaid?"

"No. The tosser she's marrying has kids. They are."

"Don't think much of him, eh?"

"I think my father thinks he wants her money. I think he's right."

"See, you and your father do agree on something." Tori smiled sadly. Thea changed the subject. "What are you wearing tomorrow?"

"I dunno."

"You know, I have a great slip dress in an apple green color that would look great on you. It has an adjustable back so I think it would fit. What are you, a 6?"

"What's that in European sizes?"

"Not sure... You want to borrow it? It has a belt if it's a little big on you."

"Could I?"

"Lets ask the goon squad if they'll bring you over early and you can get dressed at my place. I'll do your hair, too, if you want. You can come with me to the wedding, I'll be having a police escort!" They laughed.

It was a plan. They asked the big boys, and as long as Mr. Collins agreed they would have her at the Figtree Inn at 10 AM. They made their way back to the crowd, where Thea introduced Tori to her posse. Neither of them stopped dancing the rest of the night.

TEN

Jas Collins sat reclined on the built-in loveseat at the forward end of the master stateroom. He looked out at the water and the Nevis lights. He had an ice pack on his stomach and some documents he was reviewing on his lap, but his focus was elsewhere. His mind had wandered to how his life had gotten so far away from him. His daughter was a stranger to him, and a business he'd built and used to love had turned into an albatross that he seemed only to wrestle with each day. He could delegate more and not be as involved, he did trust the people he employed, but he had nothing else in his life so he worked. He worked even more as Victoria seemed to become more distant. He had no social life to speak of. He had always escorted the most beautiful single society women to events he needed to attend, but there were none that meant anything to him. He'd bedded several of them just for the release, but there were no emotional ties, on either side. Not since Nikki.

Jas met Nicola Turin through his sister Renata, which should have been his first indication that he was making a mistake. They had been the wild girls of the social circle, and Jas had been smitten with Nikki from the first time he'd seen her. She was 6 years younger than him, and had been a model when she chose to work. Her family was Swiss, and he found out later that she ran with the high priced crowd only because of her contacts through her modeling jobs, as her father was a poor pastor of a small church and her mother had died many years before. He felt sorry for her when he found out how she'd been raised, and attributed her wildness to a strict upbringing and no mother around to temper her father's fundamentalist religion. He thought that perhaps he could tame her. Nikki enjoyed Jas' attentions, and liked that he was up and coming in the business world. He was good in bed and handsome, and they made a fabulous looking couple. Her long, lean body, chestnut hair and huge gray-blue eyes and his golden boy classic looks made their photo a frequent addition to the society pages of London's papers and magazines. Jas' biggest problem with Nikki was the drugs. She did cocaine on occasion, and pot was like a glass of wine to her. He hadn't really known how bad the problem was until they'd become serious. Or as serious as Nikki ever became with anyone about anything. He'd asked her to clean up, and she promised she would, just to appease him. He thought a marriage proposal might make her take her life more seriously, and he was head over heels for this woman. Nikki said yes, not because she really wanted to be married, but she hadn't had the experience of it yet. So, yeah, why not. So they had the big society wedding with all the right people there, and were in all the magazines. Now she could say she'd experienced a wedding. And being married. How boring. She didn't really ever stop the drugs, she just did it when Jas wasn't around. And since his business was on the way up and he was a very busy man, he wasn't around a lot of the time. So Renata and Nikki were the wild girls still, only now they introduced themselves as sisters. They partied like they were single, and when Jas was around Nikki played the good wife. The only thing that slowed them down was Renata's pregnancy, at which point she married the child's father in a tight gown that showed her "problem" off to the world. Within a few months Nikki was pregnant, too. Even though she slept around, she knew it was Jas' child. He was the only one she didn't use condoms with, just her diaphragm. With the others she used both, taking no chances on either pregnancy or

AIDS. If her diaphragm had failed the only person whose sperm had a chance of reaching the target was Jas. He was elated at the news.

Nikki was not so excited. She wanted an abortion. Jas tried to convince her to have the baby. They fought long and hard about it, Nikki eventually telling Jas she was still on drugs and had been sleeping around, hoping he'd hate her enough to let her get rid of it. He did hate her at that moment, but he couldn't stop thinking about his child. She admitted to him that it was his, even Nikki wasn't that cruel. Jas made his deal with the devil. Get clean. Have the baby. You can do whatever you choose after that. Leave or stay, be a wife or not, be a mother or not. Her choice, but the baby was his. She agreed.

She lay off the drugs and alcohol and gave birth to an 6 lb. 7 oz. girl, who they named Victoria.

Nikki was all right at first after the baby was born. It was a novelty, and she even had some motherly instincts. And she also had Renata around with little Trevor to help pass the time. Jas thought that perhaps Nikki might settle down after all. He was wild about his daughter. He traveled less so he could be near her, and spent all of his free time taking care of her. His relationship with Nikki improved, even though he was still hurt and wasn't sure he'd ever really trust her again. Just after Victoria's 1st birthday and seemingly out of the blue Nikki announced she was leaving. At 24 years old she had too much life left to live to be tied down to a baby and a husband. He could have the baby, it was all he really wanted anyway, and she'd take some money and be gone. Just like that. Jas knew he shouldn't have been surprised, that was the deal they had made. But it tore him up to think this woman could walk out on this perfect little human being she'd created.

Since his wife left he'd become emotionally distant from most everyone, except Victoria, and now at 16 she was drifting away from *him*. When Nikki left, Jas' business was not the empire it is today, and she happily settled for some of his father's money just to be free. She didn't want her child, or him, and she made it quite clear she would never be back. She'd kept her promise. Even Renata didn't know whatever happened to Nikki.

When she was old enough to ask questions about her mother Jas told Victoria her mother was troubled, and that she needed her freedom to get well. He tried to make her understand that even though she couldn't see her mother, that she loved Victoria very much. He wasn't sure it was true, but he kept up appearances for the sake of the child.

And he'd never emotionally trusted a woman again, which was probably why his relationships were never more than sex.

He saw the launch approach and relaxed a little knowing Victoria would be back on board, safe. He picked up the contract he'd been reading and again tried to concentrate on it. A few moments later he heard a knock, and his door opened very quietly.

"Daddy? Are you up?"

He turned and looked toward the door, not sure if he was dreaming. She hadn't called him Daddy in three years. She stood there looking at him, chewing on her lower lip.

"Yes, come in Darling. Is everything alright?"

Tori was pleased. They'd been so much at odds recently that he hadn't called her darling in an age. She approached slowly, looking at the ice pack on his stomach, which he tried to conceal with some papers.

"It's alright. I know about the attack." Her brow was furrowed, and she looked worried. She sat on the floor next to the section on which he reclined. His expression didn't change.

"Whom do I thank for that, Duncan or Roy?" his look softened a bit.

"Neither, actually. Does it hurt? Can I see?"

Jas smiled, touched that she seemed worried about him. He was wearing drawstring pants and a gray tee shirt. She hardly ever saw him casually dressed, even on holiday. He looked so... normal. He lifted his tee shirt to show her the bruising. He was a fast healer and the bruises were already yellowing. She frowned.

"It doesn't hurt anymore. Not that I'd like to repeat the experience anytime soon."

She winced. He smiled at her, thrilled to be talking with instead of screaming at his daughter.

"You still haven't told me how you know."

"I met the woman who helped you."

Jas' face showed his surprise.

"Oh, Dad, she's brilliant. She's a photographer; she's taking photos at Aunt Rennie's wedding tomorrow. She's into music and..."

He listened to his daughter speak excitedly about her new friend. This woman had made a serious impression on Victoria, and a positive one at that. He was impressed.

"What's her name?"

"Althea Garrett. Thea actually. She took some pictures of me tonight, and said I could help her develop them tomorrow. And that I could go to the wedding with her if you'd let me go ashore in the morning. Can I, Dad?"

He hadn't seen her so happy and excited in so long he couldn't possibly refuse.

"If you take Roy with you, yes, you may go."

Tori hugged him without thinking. She felt like his little girl again, to both of them. He hugged her back, hard, and kissed the top of her head as he held her.

"I love you, Darling," He whispered.

"Oh, Daddy! I love you too." Tori thought she would cry. She pulled back a bit but stayed with her arms around his waist. He could see her lip quiver.

"I got so scared when I heard you'd been hurt. Why didn't you tell me?"

He was tempted to go into his routine about how she didn't need to know these things, but he knew they'd be screaming at each other again in no time. He was enjoying the moment too much. He sighed.

"I guess I should have. I'm sorry, pet, I didn't want you to worry."

He changed the subject by asking her about the Jump Up, and Victoria filled him in on all the people she met, how she danced all night and how great the music was.

"Oh, by the way, I brought this in for you." She searched her bag and brought out a CD. "Thea said you'd like it. That it would remind you of the Yardbirds?" She bit her lip. He laughed.

"How did she know I used to listen to the Yardbirds?"

"Well, she's almost your age, and I guess she used to."

"How old is she?" Victoria told him her comment about being 39 for 2 years now. He laughed again.

"What does she look like?" Jas asked.

"Didn't you see her the other night?"

Jas explained how she'd been behind him, and that it was almost dark and she'd had a hat on.

"She's lovely. Red hair, brown eyes, the best smile. And lots of freckles from the sun." Jas smiled at her description. He seemed to owe her a great deal, and would need to tell her tomorrow at the wedding how grateful he was.

"Why don't you put that CD in for me."

"Really?" Tori asked. Jas nodded. She inserted the disk and pressed play after finding the track Thea told her to play for him. It was The Chemical Brothers, *Let Forever Be*. The track started and the opening synthesizer sounds did bring him back to 1972. He listened for a moment. He liked it.

"Raise the volume," he told her. She grinned and cranked it, then came and sat with her back to his knee. Charles knocked loudly and Jas yelled for him to come in. Charles observed this highly unusual scene of father and daughter seemingly relaxed in each other's company and listening to very loud alternative music.

"Is everything all right, sir?" he yelled.

"Absolutely." Jas replied. Charles exited with a quizzical look on his face. Tori and her father looked at each other and laughed.

ELEVEN

Jas was amazed at how a teenager who normally slept until noon and had been up with him until after 2 AM the previous evening was bouncing around the deck at 9 in the morning harassing his men into getting her to shore. She blew him a kiss as the launch took off and yelled she'd see him later at the wedding.

Thea was waiting at the dock when the launch arrived, and gave Tori a quick hug. They stuffed Roy into the back of the Moke and took off up the hill to the Figtree Inn, passing through Charlestown and up by the baths to the high road. Roy said hello to Jett, who gave him coffee and a place to hang out where he could keep his eye on Victoria. Thea introduced Tori to Irene and Sam and then showed her around the property, ending up at her studio.

"I developed the film already. That's the boring part."

"How do you do it?" Tori seemed genuinely interested, so Thea showed her the canister, and described how the film is wound into a spool, then dropped in, and the developer is added. Tori was amazed how the first part had to be done in the dark.

"You get used to feeling it happening the right way. It takes some practice." Thea told her. She showed her the negatives. They picked the ones of Tori and began the enlargement process. As they worked Tori talked about her visit with her father the night before.

"You were right. He really liked The Chemical Brothers. He couldn't believe you picked the Yardbirds to compare them to though, he thought they sounded more like Strawberry Alarm Clock?"

Thea laughed. "I can see his point." she admitted.

"It was so brilliant, though. We talked and didn't argue. I did what you said. I didn't make faces or act smart. And I took a deep breath before I said anything. And he hugged me!"

Tori seemed so pleased.

"You know, kiddo, all relationships take work."

They printed some beautiful close ups of Tori, and Thea promised they'd mat and frame one for her father when it was dry. Thea showed her how all the equipment worked, how she could scan images into her computer and e-mail them, and even use the computer to alter some of the shots. Tori was fascinated.

They went up to Thea's room and Tori sat on the bed, looking around. She saw a picture of a cute guy on the bulletin board.

"Who's that?"

"His name is Donny Franklin."

"A bit young for you, isn't he?" Tori teased. Thea laughed. "Who is he?"

"My..." she paused and looked confused. "Um, stepson, I guess."

"Why didn't you know what to call him?" Tori asked.

"Because I wasn't ever married to his father. We lived together for 10 years. Donny's like family to me. He might be coming to visit next month before school starts."

"Why'd you break up with his dad? Or is that none of my business?" Tori asked.

"It's OK. He died in a car accident three years ago," she said.

Tori looked stricken. "How awful, I'm sorry. I didn't mean..."

"It's OK! We all have to go on when bad things happen to us." Thea smiled. "Come on, let's get some lunch."

Jett prepared curried chicken salad sandwiches and homemade breadfruit and plantain chips. They stuffed themselves and sat and talked with Irene and Sam for a while. Then they went back to Thea's room to get ready for the wedding. They had some time so Tori looked through a portfolio of Thea's work, asking questions and commenting on the ones she liked. They both took showers. Tori liked all the stuff Thea had, special shampoos and soaps and things. It was so unlike any bathroom at her house. Thea brought the dress out of the closet and displayed it for Tori, doing her best Filenes Saleswoman impression.

"I've got just the thing for you, dahling. It's you!"

Tori was laughing as she oohed and aahed over the dress. She tried it on. Thea adjusted the back straps and the skinny self-tie. Tori turned to the mirror.

"It's brilliant!"

"I agree!" Thea added. "Can I do your hair?"

"Alright." She seemed a bit wary.

Thea sat her in front of the mirror and combed her long sandy hair back away from her face. She then took strands from behind each ear and made a long, thin braid on each side. She took the two braids and wove them into a big, loose braid with the rest of Tori's hair, and fastened it at the bottom with a flat barrette. She stepped outside of her door, reached up and pinched a cluster of dark purple bougainvillea blossoms and fastened them in the barrette as well. She took the loose wisps of hair at the nape of her neck and temples and curled them into tendrils with her curling iron. The effect was very medieval, and quite stunning. Tori didn't say anything, she just smiled.

"Do you like it?" Thea asked.

"Oh, yes! Do you do makeup?" Tori asked tentatively. Thea chuckled and pulled open a whole drawer full of stuff. Tori's face lit up.

"We're going to keep this really natural, OK? No harsh lines."

Tori nodded. Thea used taupes and tans on her lids, with a gentle touch of eyeliner pencil a shade darker than Tori's lashes. She used an eyelash curler, and a light touch of brown mascara, finishing her look with a light bronze blush and a pale peach lip-gloss.

Tori was thrilled when she looked in the mirror. "I look so..."

"Grown-up. Your father's going to kill me."

They both laughed. Tori used her own jewelry, but didn't have shoes.

"What size?"

"Nine. I have huge feet."

"Young lady, I'm a 9, watch your language."

Thea found a pair of dark purple ballet flats, which fit Tori. She stood up and twirled around. She looked beautiful. Thea dressed quickly and grabbed her equipment bag on the way out. Peter was standing next to his jeep waiting for them. He whistled at Tori. She giggled. He thought Thea looked striking in her yellow capped sleeve dress. Thea motioned for Tori to sit in front, as she needed to ready some equipment and could use the space in the back seat. Roy followed in Thea's Moke. Tori looked out the window at the goats on the hillside in the hot afternoon sun, happy that Peter's Jeep was air-conditioned. She looked out over the harbor as they came down the hill and could see the launch heading toward the Island Garden hotel. As the road turned north she needed to look left to watch it, and saw Peter looking at Thea in the rear view mirror.

Thea didn't notice as she was loading cameras and organizing her bag. Peter sensed Tori's gaze and looked down at her. Tori grinned. Peter winked at her. As they reached the hotel and parked the jeep, Jas Collins was walking up the path from the marina with Duncan and Tim. Thea was standing outside the jeep with her bag on the back seat, shuffling things around. Peter offered his arm to Tori.

"Miss Collins, may I escort you to your father?" he said in a formal tone.

"Why, thank you, sir!" She took his arm and they walked toward the covered patio. Thea smiled. She watched Tori's father walk up the path. He was better looking than she'd remembered. He wore a stone colored silk three-button sport jacket with black linen pants and an off white tee shirt. He looked elegant and yet appropriately casual for the event. She could see his eyes were a piercing blue now that he was in the sunlight. His sunglasses were in his chest pocket with one of the temples stylishly hanging out. He had thick sandy gray hair that she could imagine running her fingers through. Looking at the curve of his chin and those high cheekbones gave her goose bumps. She stayed behind and watched as a surprised Jasper Collins saw his beautiful daughter.

"Who is this glorious creature, and what have you done with my child?" he asked, looking at Peter.

"Not bad for shark bait." Peter responded. They all laughed.

"Darling, you look magnificent!" He opened his arms and she hugged him. Thea was pleased. She grabbed her bag and ducked into the side entrance of the hotel to find the Guest Services Director.

Tori was really happy with her father's reaction. She twirled around for him so he could look at her, then took his arm as he asked to escort her.

"First I want you to meet Thea," she said.

"Yes, of course," he replied. They looked back where Peter's jeep was parked, but she was gone.

"She probably went in to get started with the photographs." Peter suggested. They made their way to the garden to take their seats before the ceremony.

TWELVE

Thea found Maude Thomaston, her friend and the Director of Guest Services at the Island Garden.

"Tee-a," Maude said in her very Caribbean accent, "Dis woman be a bitch."

Thea laughed. "I heard. Her niece told me all about her. Where is the blushing bride?"

Maude brought Thea to the Bridal Suite, where a 10-year-old opened the door on the first knock. Thea and Maude entered to find the suite looked like it had been under armored tank attack. Maude closed her eyes and shook her head. She whispered to Thea "She'll be telling me to make sure it is cleaned before the reception is over, I guarantee."

Renata Collins was 40 and could have been beautiful, with short blonde hair in the latest style, and her brother's piercing blue eyes. She was named after her German great grandmother on her mother's side. She could have probably had any man in the world, but she had decided the love of her life was Virgil Evans. She wasn't sure if she loved him or loved what he did for her in bed. She did know she loved that he was 30 years old and had the body of Mr. Universe. He was definitely a trophy husband. At Jasper's insistence he signed a pre-nup, although Rennie was sure she had enough of everything to keep him happy. He was a thrice-divorced father of 3 girls, all by different wives. They ranged from 10 down to 6, and Renata was planning to ship them all off to boarding school the day after the wedding. She didn't plan on any offspring with him, as she had a son by her first marriage, and they didn't have the best of relationships. He was now 17 and was staying at the hotel for the wedding. They had a relationship of convenience. When she conveniently needed to appear maternal she would send for her son. Which meant he conveniently would request money. Something had to be in it for him. Trevor O'Malley lived with his father and stepmother in Ireland, and didn't see his mother's family very often, so he was looking forward to seeing his Uncle Jas and cousin Tori that day.

Rennie Collins called to Maude and Thea from the bedroom.

"Ladies, in here." She called, oblivious to the noise of three girls and the mess around her. She was dressed and ready, putting on her lipstick. Tori's description had been apt. While her dress obviously cost a fortune, and her hair really was blonde, there was just something cheap about this woman. If British upper crust had trailer trash, she was it.

Thea introduced herself and made small talk.

"You and the young ladies look lovely," she lied, "shall we go down to the lobby and take some pictures by the fountain? Your white dresses and flowers will really stand out with the tropical colors in the background."

"Splendid idea." Rennie had plans to have these photographs in all the fashion rags. "Maude, make sure you have housekeeping clean this room before we return. Did you organize a sitter for the girls? This *is* my wedding night!"

Thea bit her lip and squeezed Maude's hand on the way by, hoping her friend would just agree and smile at the bride instead of popping her one.

The guests stood and turned to watch the bride and her attendants walk into the garden when the music began. Rennie had picked an instrumental version of Jimmy Cliff's *Many Bridges To Cross*, obviously more for the music than the lyrics. Trevor had come into the garden and found his uncle and cousin, chatting them up briefly before being called by Maude to escort his mother down the aisle. How convenient. Jas thought his sister looked as good as he'd ever seen her look, and was saddened by how that really was just damning her with faint praise. He couldn't imagine another living being so different from himself, yet they were siblings.

When the guests were seated Jas saw Althea Garrett for the first time. He was in the second row, behind his nephew, and Thea was but a few feet away, unobtrusively shooting the ceremony with her Leica. The garden was very bright and Jas had donned his shades. With his sunglasses on he could observe her unnoticed, watching her work intensely on each shot, moving gracefully about the garden. She was more beautiful than Victoria had described. He watched her red hair move as she did, skimming her shoulders and shining in the sun. He wondered what it smelled like, and had the fleeting vision of what it would be like to touch it and bury his face in it. He watched the yellow silk dress move as she walked, floating over her thighs with her movements, yet clinging just a bit suggestively to her buttocks. He watched her shining brown eyes crinkle at the corners as she smiled at the young bridesmaids sitting with his nephew, and as she lowered her camera he saw her lick her pouty lips. When he looked up to her eyes he saw she was looking at him. He removed his sunglasses and looked back at her. He smiled ever so slightly, more with his eyes than his mouth. Was she blushing? The moment was intense for him. He felt his heart beat faster.

Thea got lost in those amazing eyes. Her face got hot. What was that look? Admiration? She went back to her camera after lingering on his eyes a moment longer.

Jas continued to watch her after she looked away. She'd kept his gaze and it excited him. His mind drifted to a fantasy of her, a private moment where he rubbed his thumb over her lips, and kissed her temple and felt her hair. He was becoming aroused at his sister's wedding. He was sure there was some special karmic punishment for this.

Thea was able to take a break after the ceremony. The portrait shots had been done, and the happy couple was in their receiving line. Renata Collins-Evans didn't want a video, which made life easier, and the only shot she wanted after the service was of the cake cutting ceremony. Thea guessed she was keeping the garter. William, the bartender who counted himself as one of her posse, let Thea stash her stuff behind the bar so he could watch it for her, and gave her bottled water as she needed it. She always tipped him generously at the end of the job.

Jas Collins paused to speak with a few acquaintances from his sister's jet setting crowd who'd flown in for the nuptials. As he made his way through the party he saw Thea standing at the bar with her back to him, taking a long drink from a bottle of water. Most people were drinking champagne from the waiters' trays, so the bar was empty. He studied her beautiful backside as he approached. He took her elbow in his left hand and her right hand in his, and in a moment of pure whimsy he kissed it. She threw her head back and giggled. He smiled what she thought was the most beautiful, natural smile, one that stemmed from joy.

"Is that the way you normally introduce yourself, Mr. Collins?" she teased. Her voice was like satin gently lighting on his skin. He drank in her features.

"Based on your response I may from now on. Please, it's Jas. May I call you Thea?"

She nodded.

He looked deep into her eyes as he spoke. His eyes were smiling, like they had been in the garden. She found it exciting but very disconcerting.

"It seems I have a tremendous amount to thank you for, and an apology to give as well." His look turned more serious. "I will never forgive myself for leaving you on the beach."

"Please, don't beat yourself up over that. Your goon squad explained their position, and your response to it, shall I say? All is forgiven, I'm just glad you're OK."

"Not nearly as glad as I that you weren't hurt. I thought of nothing else until Chief Moses told me you were safe. Thank you for coming to my aid. I wished I'd actually seen what you did! Duncan described it as 'the best bloody flying kick' he'd ever seen," he said mimicking Duncan's accent. Thea laughed. William came closer to see if they wanted anything.

"What do you drink?" he asked. Thea thought it interesting that he didn't ask what she wanted, or if she wanted, he'd decided she was going to have, period.

"Bourbon."

"I love a woman who drinks bourbon," he said. He turned to William. "Do you have Knob Creek?" William nodded. "Two please, on the rocks?" He looked at Thea for approval.

She grinned and nodded. He nodded to William who began to pour.

"You do know Knob Creek is 100 proof?" she asked.

"Mm, yes, as a matter of fact I did know that."

They clinked glasses and Thea asked "To the happy couple?" Jas rolled his eyes and Thea laughed heartily. "Then how about here's to your beautiful daughter."

"I will drink enthusiastically to that." They sipped their drinks. Thea liked the way the caramel colored liquor warmed her throat and stomach on the way down, and felt like a calming salve on her nerve endings. Jas spoke again.

"Let me also thank you for spending time with Victoria. She obviously adores you and she's needed someone to talk to. I used to be that person. It's so hard now that she's…" he paused.

"A woman?" Thea offered. He winced.

"Yes." His look begged her to go on.

"You guys all crack me up. What is it you're afraid of? Do you think you're going to say or do something inappropriate? You know, I don't want to get all psychological on you here, but as an only child Tori has put all her energy into one relationship. That's what we do. When the relationship falters our lives are turned upside down. She's going through a really difficult time right now. Her hormones are a mess, she's having feelings and thoughts she doesn't understand and you're distancing yourself from her. How is she supposed to react to that?" He listened intently, leaning against the bar looking into his glass. He looked up at her with the same look of torment he had the night of the attack.

"You had a fight with her that night," Thea said without thinking as the realization came to her.

"How did you know? Did she tell you?"

"No, you just now had the same look of despair I saw on your face that night."

Her look of empathy and tenderness touched him. She reached over and gently touched his forearm. "She's still your little girl, and she needs you, probably more now than ever. Don't push her away." They looked at each other in silence for a long moment.

86

"Thank you for your candor." He smiled wistfully. "I need to work on this, we need to find some common ground."

"Play her your old Yardbirds records."

Jas laughed and the smile in his eyes came back. "That Chemical Brothers CD you recommended is brilliant. I really liked that song you suggested."

"Did you, now?" Thea understood that a change had taken place just then. She knew that what was happening now was called flirting, no question about it.

"Yes, I listened to it again today. But the next song on the track? I was almost embarrassed to be listening to it with my daughter." His eyes changed somehow.

"Why? I don't recall any graphic language on that recording." She looked puzzled. When he spoke he never took his eyes from hers.

"Because it sounded like music I'd want to make love to."

Thea felt a tingling up and down her body, and she knew the bourbon wasn't that good. Her face flushed. If this wasn't a pass she didn't know what was. She took the bait. She moved a step closer to him. The edges of his mouth began to curl as she ran the tip of her middle finger around the edge of his glass.

"I'll have to give that one another listen," she whispered. "You'll have to excuse me, they're about to cut the cake."

He moaned softly as he watched the yellow silk move over her hips as she walked away.

THIRTEEN

Jas dined with his daughter, his nephew and three friends of Renata's. The sun was sinking low and the sunset was magnificent. He was looking out for Thea Garrett, and managed to catch a glimpse of her doing a posed portrait of the bride and groom with the sunset behind them. He followed her with his eyes as he sat and sipped coffee, and was delighted when she approached the table. He stood even though she motioned for him not to get up. Trevor stood as well.

"Thea!" Tori exclaimed. "You've been so busy I haven't had time to introduce you to my dad!" She had obviously not seen them have a drink together at the bar.

"We've met," she said, giving Jas Collins a knowing look. Jas spoke.

"Thea, let me introduce my nephew, Trevor O'Malley."

"Nice to meet you Trevor, always good to know whose picture I've been taking."

They made small talk for a few moments and then Thea made a suggestion to Jas and Tori.

"May I photograph you together by the entrance to the gardens? The sunset is really amazing tonight and I think a father-daughter thing would be really beautiful. What do you say?"

They agreed, and the three of them moved to the spot. While the hotel and gardens were not on much higher ground than the beach, the vista dipped down to the ocean through a stand of palms. The low sun and the clouds reflecting the colors only seen at that time of day were magical. Thea posed them, Jas with his arm around Tori's waist and holding her other hand, his cheek near her temple. She directed them as she shot, like she would fashion models.

"Move your head to the left, Tori. Jas, look down at her. Now look at each other."

They effortlessly followed her instructions. They looked like they were engaged is a graceful dance. When Thea was finished she was excited by what she had shot.

"These are going to be great," she told them very seriously. Tori beamed.

Trevor was walking over to them and called out to his cousin.

"Tori! The DJ wants to know if we have any requests!" he yelled.

"Like he'd have anything we'd listen to!" she replied, running to catch up with him.

"That poor bastard is toast," Thea said quite seriously. Jas chuckled. He was alone with her again, and didn't want to waste the moment. He began to move toward her just as Peter Moses approached from the other side.

"I don't think it's wise for you to be this far away from the group, alone." Peter had been watching them all day. "Too many open spaces, and too much opportunity. You'll be safer closer to the other guests. Shall we?"

Jas nodded his agreement. "Of course. Thank you Peter." He offered Thea his arm. She felt amazingly awkward.

"Thank you, Jas, but I need to juggle my cameras. I'm afraid I'll need both hands."

"Let me help you," he said as he took the strap of one of the cases. She had no choice. She was doing nothing wrong, just being escorted. So why was she feeling guilty doing it in front of Peter?

They walked back to the bar. Peter moved to a place where he could observe the whole area, and Thea put her cameras away, technically finished for the evening. As she turned around Jas Collins handed her another glass of Knob Creek.

"Oh, God. Are you trying to get me pissed so you can take advantage of me?" she said, laughing.

"Will it work?"

"Nope."

He smiled. "That wasn't entirely my intent. But I reckoned I could at least get you to stay and chat with me if I bought you a drink."

"Deal."

They sat down at the bar, knee to knee.

"Do you have to run off?" he asked.

"No, but usually the hired help doesn't get to stay and partake of the festivities."

"Have you eaten?" He looked concerned for her welfare. She was amused.

"My man, William here took care of me." She smiled at the handsome young black man behind the bar.

"William, what did she have for dinner?"

William chuckled. "Her usual." Jas looked at him quizzically.

"What would that be?"

"A grilled cheese and chutney sandwich."

Jas smiled. "I didn't think you could get something like that in a place like this."

William enlightened him. "Miss Thea gets anything she wants in my establishment, sir." He was talking as though he owned the place, grinning.

Thea excused herself and headed to the powder room. Tori caught up with her.

"Are you having fun?" Thea asked.

"Oh, yeah! You aren't going to leave, are you? I saw you packing up."

"No, not yet. Your father bought me a drink, so I'll be sitting with him for awhile."

"The DJ actually has some good music!" Tori said. "But Trevor doesn't like to dance, so I guess it doesn't matter."

"Why don't you ask your father?"

Tori laughed. "I've never seen him dance in my life!" she exclaimed.

"I bet he does." Thea thought of how gracefully he moved, and ran. Her face flushed thinking of how men who are good dancers are usually great in bed. "Promise me something? Two things."

Tori nodded.

"Number one: that you'll ask your father to dance."

Tori agreed.

"Number two: that you won't marry a man who can't dance." Tori squealed with laughter as Thea smiled at her.

When they returned to the bar Jas Collins was standing a short distance away in conversation with his sister. She looked down her nose at Thea as she sat at the bar and picked up her drink. Rennie began to move toward her, as though she would dismiss her for the evening when Jas caught her arm. Tori's eyes got wide and Thea turned her head for fear of laughing when they heard him say to his sister:

"Althea Garrett is an old friend of mine and she'd agreed to stay as my guest here this evening. You don't have a problem with that, do you Rennie?" His voice was smooth and cold. She feigned a sweet smile.

"Of course not. Enjoy!" she said as she trounced off.

Thea was amused at his charade, and it gave her the opportunity to stay a while longer.

The DJ switched from the mellow dinner music by announcing that it was time to party to the beginning strains of the Talking Heads' *Burning Down the House*. Thea raised her eyebrows to Tori, signaling her to go for it. Tori smiled and as her dad approached she caught his hand.

"Dance with me?" He looked stunned and delighted. He took off his jacket and laid it over the barstool, smiling at his daughter. He cast Thea a glimpse with those playful, smiling eyes and walked his daughter to the dance floor.

Thea thought to herself, "*Ah, just as I thought, an Alpha Male who wouldn't waste a chance to show off his feathers.*" She continued to smile as she watched them. She'd seen Tori dance the night before, but wasn't sure Jas had ever seen his daughter on a dance floor. They began to move to the music. He was good. He was not only good he was hot. Sexy, fluid, strong, masculine all came to mind. No wonder all women want to mate the Alpha Male. Tori kept casting Thea looks that communicated her amazement.

When the song ended Thea applauded very enthusiastically for father and daughter.

They were both still smiling when they reached her.

"Ladies," he said as he slipped his arm around his daughter, "I can't remember the last time I had this much fun." Tori hugged him. Trevor called her and she slipped from his arm and was off. Thea and Jas were beginning to flirt again when the next song was coming to a close and the DJ made an announcement.

"The next song is a shout out to Thea and Dad from Tori."

Thea blushed. Jas' smile spread slowly. They heard the first guitar riff of The Yardbirds' *Heart Full of Soul* and both began to laugh. He grabbed her hand and dragged her to the dance floor. They moved the moves of their youth, Thea even went so far as to do the pony. Tori joined them on the floor, laughing and trying to copy Thea's motions. She laughed with a mixture of joy and embarrassment when her father sang the refrain to her in front of everyone. He actually had a great voice, to both Thea and Tori's delight. He grabbed his daughter and twirled her around as the song ended.

"You do a mean pony, Althea," he said to her as they reached the bar.

"You cut the rug pretty good there yourself, my friend. When's the last time you went dancing?" she asked. He paused a moment.

"I can't remember."

"Jasper Collins, you need to have more fun."

"Walk with me."

They strolled through the hotel lobby so Peter wouldn't feel the need to chase them back to the crowd.

"When was the last time you went dancing?" he asked her.

"Last night."

"Ah, the jump up. Do you go every week?" he asked.

She nodded.

"Thea, what are you doing here? How did you come to live on a Caribbean Island?"

She thought about how to answer.

"I had a crisis of faith, and my life didn't fit anymore. I had to simplify things in order to resolve it." They were both quiet for a moment.

"Have you? Resolved it, I mean?" he asked.

"Mostly. It sneaks up on me sometimes. The middle of the night can be difficult."

He wasn't prying, and he was comfortable to talk with. She went on and told him about her parents and then Kip.

He mumbled, "Oh my God" and then was silent.

"So, I needed to understand why I was here. What my purpose was, what I might have been atoning for with these tests of faith."

"Do you know?" he said, with a sideways glance.

"Not really. I'm not sure I ever will. Maybe I needed to come here to help a really wonderful guy repair his relationship with his teenage daughter." She smiled.

They found themselves on a balcony overlooking the golf course, with a trellis of bougainvillea that was illuminated by the moon. A gecko skittered past on the railing.

"Hearing someone else's problems makes your own seem insignificant," he remarked quietly.

"If I have any advice to give to anyone, it's to appreciate everything you can. Family, friends, life! It's too precious, and way too short. So I try to enjoy as much as I can. I had to sort this all out and I needed time, so I came here. It's not forever, but it's good right now."

"Thank you for telling me. I hope it wasn't too horrible talking about it," he said softly.

She shook her head. He took her hands before he spoke.

"I think I have a better perspective of my daughter since I've met you. I really do feel I owe you a great debt."

"Not to mention that I can drop would be attackers with a single kick." She roused them from their serious discussion with her comment.

"You could be remarkably handy to have around," he joked.

"Speaking of that, do you have any idea why anyone would try to hurt you? Was it an attempted kidnapping, do you think?"

"No. I think I was being sent a message. A company I've bid on in the states is afraid I'll close their unionized warehouse and, well it's complicated."

"World Markets is afraid you'll close the Chicopee facility and negotiate a service contract with S&C Wholesale in Bennington?" she asked. He was stunned. She continued.

"Everyone's known for years that the damned union shop has been breaking them. S&C's been courting them for years. They're ripe for becoming an indirect buying account. You know, I don't know who's done the due diligence for you, but I hope they've seen the trends with chains that close warehouses. It's not pretty."

He was fascinated. "How so?"

"Look at Homeland, Grocers Junction, Robertson's and B&P in New England alone. They closed their warehouses and contracted with wholesalers because they already had money problems. It was the beginning of the end. They've all been absorbed or sold off in pieces. Is that what you have planned for World Markets?"

"It needs an infusion of capital if it's going to survive. I can do that." He looked at her intently. "Who are you? Or should I ask, who were you in your other life?"

"I was Northeast Division Manager for the NEAU Grower's Cooperative. Um, that's the New England Agricultural Union. I did business with all the classes of trade that sell groceries in the Northeast Corridor." She smiled.

"I may have you look at the World Markets business plan," he said.

"Be happy to. We should get back before Peter sends the cavalry."

They began walking back.

"Would you do me the honor of being my guest on the yacht?" he asked.

"Oh, um. When? Aren't you leaving soon? Tori told me."

He interrupted her. "We were. Leaving that is. But I've changed my mind. Victoria never gets to see Trevor, and he's joining us for a few days. I haven't told her yet, but he may have by now. I thought we might cruise to Anguilla. Join us?" He was serious.

"Why the change of plans?"

"I'm not going to let the union organizers, if that's who it was, run my life. If I do that, they win. And I recall someone telling me I need to have more fun."

She laughed.

"Say yes."

"OK, yes."

He smiled that beautiful smile again, offered her his arm and escorted her back to the fete.

FOURTEEN

Peter had watched Thea and Jas Collins together for most of the evening. They seemed to have a great deal to discuss, and seemed happy to discuss it. When Thea made her excuses and left the party, Jas Collins had walked her to her mini Moke. Peter wondered what might have happened if he had not arrived to follow her home in his Jeep. Jas had kissed her hand and gone back to the patio. Peter tailed Thea back to the Figtree Inn and pulled up beside her as she got out of her vehicle.

"Are you going straight to bed?" he asked.

"Yeah," she said, "I have an early day tomorrow. Why?" she asked. Peter smiled.

"No! Peter," she whispered, "this was supposed to be a once in awhile thing. You just saw me on Wednesday."

"But I can't help thinking about you when I see you all day."

"Well, then you'll have a break this week. I'm joining Jas Collins and his daughter on the yacht tomorrow. I'll be gone for a few days."

"Thea! The man might be a target. That is not a wise move!"

"I can't live my life worrying about what might happen," she said emphatically.

Peter just shook his head. "Be careful," he said tersely as he put the jeep in reverse and sped off.

Thea stood and watched him go. She felt sad. She wasn't sure if it was because Peter was her friend and he was obviously not pleased with her, or if it was because she realized that what they had really was over.

Thea awoke early the next day and developed the film from the wedding. She would have time to print proofs and drop them by the hotel for Renata Collins-

Evans before she met the launch from The Victoria at the dock. She really wanted to see the photos she'd taken of Jas and Tori. She had a feeling they would be special.

She packed a bag for her excursion, finished up in the lab and labeled the proofs. She showered and dressed in a sundress, and said goodbye to Irene and Sam before heading off. She had no more jobs for 10 days, and hadn't heard back from Donny as to if or when he was visiting. She met Maude at the hotel and gave her the book of proofs to forward to the happy couple and quickly drove to the docks, hoping she wasn't running late.

Trevor O'Malley was there with his bag, and the launch was approaching as she walked onto the dock. Duncan helped them both on and quickly turned back toward The Victoria. Thea loved being on the ocean. She didn't care if it was a sailboat or motor powered, the smell of the salt and the wind in her hair exhilarated her. She always said she could die a happy woman after a day out at sea.

She got a good look at the yacht as they drew closer. She guessed it was about 150'. It was a glorious specimen. There was a heli-pad on the top deck, but no helicopter was positioned there that day. She'd never spent any time on something this luxurious, and she was very curious about it's amenities.

Tori and her father were there to greet their guests, although Jas waved from afar as he talked on the phone, obviously trying to end the conversation. He looked handsome in navy pants and a gold colored polo shirt. Tori gave Thea a hug, and Roy took Thea and Trevor's bags and disappeared below deck. Jas joined them shortly after. He shook Trevor's hand, and took both Thea's hands and kissed her on the cheek. She smiled at him.

"Hi," she said simply.

"Welcome," he said, the smile flooding his eyes. He looked into her eyes a moment longer, just enough to make her flesh tingle. "I'm so glad you're here."

"Thank you for asking me," she said quietly. "Do I get a tour?"

"Absolutely."

The yacht's horn sounded to signal that they would be underway. He brought her everywhere on the ship, showed her the bridge, the galley, the wine cellar, his office and finally they found themselves below decks where the staterooms were. He pointed out Tori's room, where she and Trevor were already listening to music and looking at each other's CDs. He showed her the room where he had instructed Roy to put Trevor's bag, an empty stateroom, and then her room, which was next door to his.

"This is great, I'll be very happy here," she said enthusiastically. He took her hand and led her into the next door, his door. The master stateroom had a king sized bed, where all the others had twins. There was a built in sofa three steps up from the floor level where you could sit and be at eye level with the ocean. Where there was no glass to look out there were bookshelves. There was a built in bar, a stereo system and big screen TV, and a private bath with a Jacuzzi and sauna. She stood and drank it all in.

She hadn't heard the door close behind her.

"Do you like this better? I'd love to share it with you," he asked softly as he walked up very close behind her.

"Behave yourself. I can still swim from here." She was smiling as she turned to face him.

He was grinning but she felt his look was more serious than his smile betrayed. She looked in his eyes a little too long, and was helpless when he pulled her toward him and wrapped his arms around her, finding her mouth with his. He kissed her deep and hard, massaging her back. She realized she'd wanted him to kiss her since last night. He was lost in her. He felt a passion that had been gone from his life for a long time. He wanted her, but he was afraid of the emotions he felt. He pulled back and looked at her. She sensed his uneasiness, and gave him an escape.

"Jas, do you think this is wise?"

"What do you mean?" He was fearful of his feelings but she was so damned beautiful.

"If this is just... just a fling, how will Tori feel? She'll have hopes that we're something more and she'll be crushed if we aren't. As much as I would like..." She paused. "Maybe we shouldn't risk it," she said quietly.

"I hadn't thought of it like that." He had his arms around her and her forehead rested on his chin.

"How about we just enjoy each other's company for awhile?" she suggested.

He looked down at her. She was so comfortable to be around.

"What if we feel like there is more?" he asked.

"How about we give it some time? Maybe you'll want to throw me overboard in a couple of days."

He smiled. "I'll behave, but it's against my better judgment." He still had his arms around her. She reached up and stroked his cheek, tenderly kissed his lips and pulled away.

"That's not fair," he said, as he watched her move out the door.

Thea wandered up the stairs and moved out into the air aft of the forward observation deck. An older man dressed in a jacket approached her.

"You must be Ms. Garrett. Please allow me to introduce myself. I am Charles Marston, Mr. Collins' secretary." He offered his hand. She shook it and smiled at him.

"Nice to meet you, Mr. Marston."

"I hope your stay with us will be pleasurable. Please let me know if there is anything you require."

"Thank you, sir."

He was impressed at her respectfulness. Most guests on this ship called him Chuck or Charlie or Charles if he was lucky. But most guests were American Businessmen who were lacking in social skills as far as he was concerned.

"How long have you worked for Mr. Collins, Mr. Marston?" she asked.

"Oh, my. Twelve years I believe, and I worked for the senior Mr. Collins before that. I have been in service to this family for twenty two years in total." He beamed proudly.

Thea questioned him about his duties to the senior Mr. Collins, were they in the same business, did he accompany Jas Collins everywhere. The older man happily opened up to her, discussing his position at length, enjoying their interaction immensely. He was impressed by her interest in him and her sincere demeanor. He finally realized he was acting like a guest himself.

"Miss Garrett, I have been babbling on. Do forgive me. It has been a pleasure, though. May I offer you anything? A glass of wine, perhaps?"

"I would love a glass of bottled water."

He directed her to a deck chair and returned shortly after with a goblet of iced water with a lemon slice, and the rest of the bottle. He placed it on the side table next to her. She thanked him.

"I hope we have an opportunity to speak further, Mr. Marston."

"Thank you, Miss Garrett. So do I."

Charles met Jas on the way through the forward observation deck, and informed him of Miss Garrett's whereabouts.

"That most delightful young woman that you have invited on board is on the sundeck." Charles' expression was characteristically serious. Jas smiled at him.

"Gotten to you, too, has she?" Charles uncharacteristically looked a bit flustered.

"I mean no offense, sir, but those horrid business people you so often entertain are gutter slime in comparison."

Jas laughed out loud as Charles continued to his office. Jas found Thea out on deck, the wind blowing her hair. The sun made her red hair a fiery color. He stood and watched her for a while before he grabbed a bottle of seltzer from the bar and walked to join her. She was leaning on the rail, watching the ocean move past. He leaned against her, arm to arm and followed her gaze.

"What do you see?" he asked.

"Water," she quipped.

He looked at her with a grin. "May I be so forward as to ask you to look at the business plan for World Markets? You mentioned you wouldn't mind."

"Like I said, I'd be happy to. Should we do it now?"

"If you'd care to. If you'd rather stay out here and enjoy the sun it can wait."

She motioned with her head toward the stairs, and they made their way toward his office. She detoured to her stateroom and met him there. He sat her at his desk and put the file in front of her. It was an impressive presentation, with many appendices, including photographs of the flagship stores. She took out her tortoiseshell glasses and put them on. Jas immediately had a librarian fantasy. He could imagine kissing her and undressing her, touching her while she moaned with pleasure until the only thing she had left on were those glasses. He turned and looked out at the ocean so she wouldn't see the activity happening in his groin, and told himself to get a grip.

"This is gonna take awhile, if you have something else you want to do." she said as she looked over the tops of the frames. He was under control enough to turn and face her. "Can I have a pad and pen to make notes?" she asked.

"Of course," he said as he walked to her and opened a drawer. "I'll leave you to it. Charles' call button is on the phone. Let him know if you need anything, or when you're through. He'll find me."

She leaned back in his big, leather chair and tucked her legs up underneath her. He watched her for a moment as she tapped the end of his Mont Blanc pen on her lips while she studied the page. As he left the room he realized it was going to be very difficult to have her so nearby and not be able to touch her.

FIFTEEN

Tori and Trevor came up on deck and found Tori's dad.

"Where's Thea?" she asked.

"She's in my office. She agreed to look over a business plan for me."

"You invited her on holiday and are making her work?"

Jas could see a screaming match in the making. He forced himself to relax his shoulders, took a deep breath and grabbed his daughter in a hug and swung her around.

She giggled with pleasure.

"No, Miss Nosey, I'm not making her do anything. Did you know Thea was in my line of business before she came to Nevis?"

"No. Yes! She mentioned the food business the night I met her."

"She knows a lot about the company I'm bidding on. And she offered to look at the plan. I have not enslaved her." He kept his demeanor light, hoping his daughter would do the same. "She's been down there for awhile. Would you like to go and rescue her?" he asked.

"Yes, I'll be right back."

Tori entered her father's office to find Thea busily jotting notes on a legal pad. She looked over her glasses as the door opened.

"You need to come up for air," Tori said. Thea chuckled.

"Yes, you're right, I do. I'm just about done anyway so your timing is perfect." Thea gathered up her notes and the plan in a folder and followed Tori above deck. The galley crew had brought up a tray of hors d'oeuvres, and Trevor was busy munching on a wedge of cheese. Jas smiled at them as they entered the observation deck and plopped down on the divan.

"Drink?" he queried. She nodded enthusiastically. He walked behind the bar and poured two glasses of Knob Creek bourbon over ice. He came to her and handed her one as he sat next to her. They clinked glasses and both took a swallow.

"Oh, I almost forgot," she said. "I need to run below, I brought something for you and I left it in my stateroom."

"I'll go!" Tori said, heading for the steps.

"Bring the canvas bag on the bed? Thank you."

"So, dare I ask what you learned about World Markets?" Jas inquired.

"Well," she began, "let me preface this by saying I can only comment on the parts of the business I'm familiar with. There's a lot I don't know about running a chain. I do know about things like supply side, logistics and activity based costing."

Trevor looked over and said "What language are you speaking?" Thea laughed.

"If I were you, I'd have my accountants look into the percent of sales they claim the warehouse is costing them to maintain. It looks very low to me. If they were that efficient there is no way the union would be concerned about a warehouse closing and a move to a grocery wholesaler. I know what a nightmare account they were because of their tight warehouse space, and how often they refused trucks that they needed because they had no place to put them and were at the mercy of the union when it came to contracting for outside storage."

"How so?"

"If we sent a cross dock pallet, in other words, a pallet that could go right out onto the selling floor of the account, they didn't have to take it into inventory. They just had to stick it on their own truck and send it out to a store. It was a money and labor saving opportunity. Because the union wanted to make sure their people touched every load going to the stores, they required that product in outside storage be brought back to the regular picking warehouse prior to going to a store. Even cross-docks, which could have been delivered to the stores directly from outside storage had to make an extra stop at the pick warehouse. It took all the labor and dollar savings out of the program. I know they are not efficient logistically, and I know S&C, the grocery wholesaler that's been courting them, has contracts with indirect buying customers that aren't as good as World Markets says their facility costs to operate. It's impossible for them to be that efficient. S&C subsidizes their low-balled contracts with money they extort from their vendors."

"Continue," he said, weighing this information.

"They disguise it as a 'partnering' program. For a percentage of sales, you get them to not buy your product from diverters, a warehouse withdrawal report on all your items to their various indirect buying accounts, some useless category management reports, and advance notice of deductions they might take from invoices paid. The only value, as I see it, is to keep them from diverting."

Jas knew of the practice of diverting. It meant a customer with an attractive promotional deal on a product line would sell it to a customer in another part of the country whose deal wasn't as good. The problem was more that a vendor's salespeople and food brokers weren't compensated for the cases that came into their market through diverting. Also, the promotional deal had been paid to the original customer who purchased the product. If the customer that bought diverted goods ran a performance, he, too, expected to be paid. The vendor ended up paying for advertising and price reductions on the same goods twice. It was a big problem for national manufacturers.

Thea continued. "But a chain has no such partnering program, unless they're grossly overcharging for promotional fees, like the cost of ads. Or if they're charging nuisance fees, like $500 for non-notification of a coupon dropping in the marketplace, stuff like that. The other issue I would take up is on the activity based costing. They claim the cost of conditioning the shelf is far lower than I've seen it in any efficiency presentation. They don't case pack the shelves, they don't use bins to dump product into, and they don't sell a lot of multi pack, shrink-wrapped items. They don't have a limited assortment, either. It's gotta be costing them more to physically stock the shelves than that line item states. You might also look and see what their market development funds were last year vs. this year. If the vendors are withholding funds it's because the chain isn't efficient."

"I never considered that," he rubbed his chin.

"And if the funding was the same, research what price points they ran on like items. They may have taken a gross profit margin hit just to make their promotions look more successful. The industry analysts would probably have a handle on that, so your people might already have the info." She paused and took a sip of her drink. "Anyway, I took notes that I think you can figure out. They're all here."

"Thea, I can't thank you enough. This is very valuable data."

"Your people might already know all this." she tried to downplay her contribution.

"If they do, and believe me they'll be the first to let me know, then I'll be very impressed by them. If they don't, then perhaps I'll have to hire new ones."

Thea wasn't sure if he was serious or not.

"Please tell me you don't manipulate people's lives so casually." It would distress her to no end if he were a fat cat that didn't care what happened to his rank and file.

Ah, he thought to himself, she is a champion of the proletariat. Tori returned with the bag.

"Victoria, tell Thea what we did last Christmas in New York."

"Oh, it was brilliant. We rented out the whole Radio City Music Hall for the Christmas Show one night and dad flew all his employees and their families in for the show and a big party."

"Do I know every employee in the company personally? No, of course not. But I do know the name the mailroom clerk in our San Francisco office. It's Ming Jeffries, and she's leaving on maternity leave next month," he added.

Thea was embarrassed. She was ready to brand him as a corporate villain, when he was really probably a very good man. She knew her face was red.

"I am sorry," she said, staring at a spot on the rug, not able to meet his eyes.

"Which corporate giant caused you to believe that all high level management is soulless? For whom did you work?" he asked gently.

She looked at him tentatively. She told him a name.

"Good God, no wonder you were so quick to brand me as Satan. How long were you in their employ?"

"Six years."

"And how many years of therapy has it taken for you to recover?" he joked. She still looked uncomfortable. Tori was watching, feeling bad for her friend but not really sure what this was all about.

"Thea, I'm not perfect, but I do care about what happens to my people. Only with trust and respect do I feel I'll ever attract quality workers to my businesses." He leaned his forearms on his knees and took her hand and she looked at him. "I really was just joking before, no one's going to get fired."

"Oh, I'm such an idiot," she said. She smiled at him. "Please accept my apology."

"None was required." He squeezed her hand.

She really wanted to change the subject. She exhaled audibly and opened the bag Tori brought.

"Tori, come sit here." She moved to let the girl sit between she and Jas. She handed them a book of proofs that were of the two of them at the wedding. They opened the cover and Tori gasped.

"Thea, these are awesome!" She was delighted; they looked like two fashion models yet you could feel the warmth between them in every shot. Thea looked at Jas as he studied each page. Father and daughter looked very much alike. He was intensely focused on the book. Finally he looked up. His expression was one of gratitude and amazement.

"How can I ever thank you? May I order copies from you? Victoria, we want all of them, don't you agree?"

"Jas, stop it. I will make as many of whatever size you'd like. My pleasure."

"May I use one in our annual report?"

"Well, that's gonna cost ya," she joked.

Jas was glad the tension in the room had begun to disperse.

After a gourmet dinner in the formal dining room the foursome had dessert out on the deck in the cool evening air. Charles interrupted with a message for Jas, who excused himself. Thea was left with Tori and Trevor.

"Hey you guys, come with me." She motioned for them to follow her up to the helicopter pad. She walked to the middle and sat down, patting the fiberglass on each side of her, signaling them to sit.

"OK, lay back and look at the stars."

Out in the middle of the Caribbean with no lights around, the sky looked vast.

"Wow," said Tori.

"Bloody amazing," echoed Trevor.

They pointed out the very obvious constellations to each other and realized laughingly that none of them knew a great deal about astronomy. Thea suggested an experiment.

"OK, look at the stars and think of them as though they were below you instead of above you. Like you were hanging upside down and you could fall into them. Really concentrate."

All was quiet for several minutes until she heard Trevor's hands slap the deck hard followed by Tori's. Thea laughed like crazy.

"Did you fall out?" she asked. Both kids were sitting up looking at her and each other wide-eyed. Thea laughed again at their expressions.

Jas had come on deck and heard the laughter above. He walked up to see the three of them laughing and Trevor and Tori shaking their heads in amazement.

"What's going on?" he asked.

"Dad, come here. You have to try this." Tori pulled him down next to Thea. He turned to look at her.

"OK, look at the stars," Thea said, and then went on to give him the same instructions as she did Trevor and Tori. The kids laid back down so as not to be in his line of vision. Jas stared at the stars, looking at the blackness that enveloped them and began to envision he was looking down into them. He concentrated very hard. As he did he got the feeling that he wasn't really attached to anything, his body, the ship, anything. It was as though he was falling down into the night. It frightened him. He jerked himself back, and he too slapped the deck with both hands. Thea, Tori and Trevor laughed uproariously. Jas sat up, eyes wide.

"What was that?" he said as he started to chuckle. He was looking down at Thea who was still lying on the deck.

"Did you feel like you do when you're falling in a dream?" she asked.

"Yes, that's it exactly!" Tori said.

"Some people say that our spirits travel when we sleep, and that falling feeling is when we come back to our bodies. I was told you could also consciously leave by doing the exercise you all just did. I've never gotten any farther than you just did, but it's very exciting, don't you think?" Thea asked.

They sat around discussing it while Jas just looked at Thea. How did this outrageous and wonderful creature find her way into his life?

SIXTEEN

Everyone was in bed by 11, alone, much to Jas' dismay. He had respectfully not made another advance toward her. Partly because she had asked him to give their friendship some time, and partly because he really was afraid to trust again. She was warm and funny, and amazingly easy to be around. She was intelligent, had a conscience, and was personable to everyone. Victoria adored her. And she was beautiful and sexy. There had to be a catch. Perhaps he was smitten because he knew just now that he couldn't have her. Perhaps if their relationship turned physical his feelings toward her would change.

He thought about the fact that he was having feelings at all. That in itself seemed a minor miracle. He fell asleep thinking of holding Thea in his arms.

The morning light awoke Thea, but the sun had not appeared yet. Where were they? she thought. She threw on a leotard and a pair of nylon shorts, piled her hair on top of her head, brushed her teeth and washed her face, grabbed a towel and headed up on deck. She met a cabin boy on her way through the main salon and had a short chat with him. He informed her they were anchored off Anguilla's shore.

Thea went up to the heli-pad with her towel and looked around to get her bearings. She saw a road on a steep incline, and the high cliffs of what might be South Hill. That's why there was no sun in this clear blue sky, it hadn't topped the hill yet. If that was South Hill then they were anchored in Sandy Ground. She scanned the beach area. There was Johnno's! They were in Sandy Ground!

Thea loved Anguilla. She thought that if she ever bought a place in the Caribbean it would be there. Nevis

112

was lush and beautiful, but Anguilla's snorkeling and beaches were the best. She'd put up with the flat and arid inland areas to be able to walk into the azure waters and snorkel right off shore.

She took a deep breath and raised her arms above her and began her routine.

Jas got up and threw on a pair of running shorts and a tee shirt, made a quick trip to the bathroom to splash water on his face and make sure he looked halfway decent. He headed up on deck to grab a cup of coffee. He could have called and had someone bring it to his stateroom, but he was restless this morning, though he wasn't sure why. As he entered the hall he saw that Thea's door was open and her bed was made. How odd, he thought. Had she not slept in it? Had he dreamt her, was she never here at all?

He checked Victoria's room to see if maybe she'd bunked in there. In typical teenage fashion Victoria was a heap in a jumble of bedclothes. He pulled the door closed. It was 6:15 in the morning. Where was she? He headed up on deck. One of the cabin boys was walking through the observation room, heading toward the sundeck with a tray.

"Good morning Mr. Collins."

"Good morning Brian," he began. "Have you seen Miss Garrett this morning?"

"Yes, sir. She came upstairs and asked where we were. I told her we were off Anguilla's shore, and asked if I could get her breakfast and make up her cabin for her." He paused.

"And?" Jas encouraged him to continue.

"She said she'd tidied up her cabin already and would just need some fresh towels. I haven't done that yet, sir."

"That's fine, please continue."

"Then she asked for some strong black coffee, and perhaps some yogurt and fruit if it wasn't too much trouble." Brian motioned to the Thermos pot and the covered dish on the tray.

Jas smiled at Thea's considerate nature and at the amount of information the young man felt the need to give him. Brian went on.

"She said she wouldn't need it for half an hour or so, but I thought I'd have it ready for her when she was done."

"Done doing what?" Jas asked.

"Not sure exactly, sir. But she had on exercise clothes and had a towel, and she headed up to the helicopter pad."

"Now we're getting somewhere."

"I'd guess she was exercising, sir."

"I'd say you're probably right. How long ago was that, Brian?"

"About 15 minutes or so. Can I get you some coffee, sir?" the young man asked.

"Bring another cup and I'll share hers. Thank you Brian"

Jas headed up the steps to the heli-pad. His bare feet made no sound, and he moved more slowly as he saw her. She was in the middle of a yoga routine that she obviously knew very well. He sat on the top step and watched her move from one pose to the next, listened to her controlled breathing, and watched the muscles stretch and relax. Her eyes were closed and her face serene as she slid her limbs into each position. She looked as though she were in a moving meditation, or praying. It was beautiful. She moved gracefully from a cat stretch to a standing position, lifting her arms to the sides like an angel spreading her wings as she inhaled. Her hands met above her head, and prayer-like, she moved them down past her face, stopping at chest level as she exhaled.

At that moment the sun peeked over the cliffs and illuminated her face. She looked up and opened her eyes. The delight she felt flooded her eyes and her smile spread across her face as she whispered, "How beautiful."

"I was just thinking the same thing," he whispered, looking at her from his perch on the steps. She looked over at him, surprised, but then smiled broadly as she felt the blush rise on her face.

"Pay homage to the sun and it appears," he said.

"Interesting choice of words," she replied.

"That's what it looked like. A prayer. Or perhaps a meditation."

"How long have you been sitting there?" she asked.

"About ten minutes. I wish I'd found you sooner." He smiled at her and she saw that fire in his eyes that made her heart beat faster.

She grabbed her towel and sat down next to him.

"Do you do yoga every morning?" he asked.

"I try. I sometimes lack discipline," she laughed. "Do you work out?" *or does that amazing body just come naturally*, she thought to herself.

"I run when I can. I do some weight training when I'm at home. I bring resistance bands when I travel," he said.

"You're welcome to join me," she said, smiling.

"Based on what I just witnessed I think my muscles would snap."

"Do you stretch after you run?"

"Um, sometimes," he said guiltily.

"Yeah, yeah, typical man."

"Hey!" he jibed.

"May I teach you two stretches you can do every morning to ease yourself into the day?" she asked. He smiled at the thought of having her as his personal trainer. Another fantasy came to mind.

"OK," he said. She moved to the center of the deck and motioned him over.

"Lay on your back." He did, as she went to her knees next to him. "Pull your right leg to your chest, hands under your thigh."

He thought how he'd rather have his hands under her thigh.

"Stretch your left leg, and point your toes. Good. Now pull your right leg over your left. Use your left arm to help if you want." She pulled his leg over gently to show him.

Now, turn your head to face right, and extend your right arm on the floor at shoulder level. This is called the morning star. Now relax." They heard small cracking noises.

"Was that me?" he asked.

"Yes. Ever been to a chiropractor?" she asked. He shook his head. "Same thing," she joked. "OK, now bring your knee back slowly and rest the ankle on your left knee. Good. Now grab your left thigh and bring it toward your chest. This stretches your lower back and buttocks."

"This feels great." She made him repeat it on the other side, where they heard the same cracking noises.

"What is that?" he asked.

"Your sacroiliac joint is just making itself more comfortable. Not to worry."

She then showed him a sitting stretch for his upper back and neck. He was really enjoying this.

"My hamstrings are what usually are tight," he commented. She instructed him to sit with his legs straight in front.

"Pull up tall, inhale and reach forward over your legs. Don't round over," she instructed.

He was pretty limber, she commented to herself. As he stretched forward she got behind him and leaned her chest on his back, hands on the floor next to his thighs. He really liked this part.

"Exhale," she said. As he did, she gently allowed her weight to push him further forward, deepening his stretch. He couldn't believe how much farther he was able to stretch. She made him hold it for about 15 seconds and then release it.

"That was amazing," he said. "I've never been able to stretch so far."

"That's from not stretching when you run," she admonished. He playfully stuck his tongue out at her. She regretted her quick comeback after it passed her lips. "Is that all the French you know?" she joked.

That was all he needed. He hadn't stopped thinking about touching her, and now she was touching him while teaching him to stretch, he could smell her, she was too close and he couldn't stand it any more. He snatched her into his arms and pulled her on top of him as he sat. She giggled and squirmed in his arms.

"You want French?" he asked, "I'll give you French." He rolled them over on their sides and clutched her close to him as he hungrily closed his mouth over hers. He kissed her feverishly as he moved his hands over her back and wrapped his leg over her so she couldn't escape. She had slid her arms around his neck and was running her fingers through his thick hair as she kissed him back. Who was she kidding? She wanted him and was thrilled to be kissing him, her resolve to not hurt his daughter growing weaker.

They were making out like two teenagers in the backseat of a car. He had no feelings of fear as he kissed her this time. He just wanted her, and he was enjoying having this delightful woman in his arms. He pulled back and looked at her. Her hair comb had fallen out and her hair was a tumble of waves around her face. He kissed her again, gently, and then whispered to her.

"I don't want to keep my hands off of you." He was serious.

"I don't want you to," she whispered back. Permission granted. He kissed her again, holding her face and stroking her hair.

He got up, pulling her with him and they made their way down three flights, trying to avoid running into anyone. They managed to sneak into his stateroom unnoticed, and he quickly locked the doors. She stood at the other end of the cabin.

"How late will the kids sleep?" she whispered.

"Noon," he replied with a grin.

"Will anyone be looking for you?" she asked. He took the phone out of the cradle and dialed.

"Charles, yes, good morning. No calls, no interruptions, right. Thank you." He replaced the receiver to end the call, thought about it and took it off the hook. He looked up at her.

She looked... uncomfortable. He approached her gingerly and took her hands.

"What's wrong?" he asked. She shook her head and smiled.

"Just nervous."

"About what?" he asked as he gently stroked her arms with his fingertips. She shrugged and shook her head. He smiled as he slipped his hands around her waist and pulled her to him. He kissed her temple and her earlobe, smelled her hair and kissed her neck, murmuring to her while he worked his way to her shoulder.

"Oh. Thea, you are so lovely. All I've been able to think about is holding you and making love to you. Since I first saw you in the garden, I've wanted you," he rubbed his thumb on her lower lip and she kissed it gently. Arousal had taken her over and he had done nothing more than kiss her and talk to her. She wanted him, and he was being a gentleman and letting her slowly become comfortable with him. Or was this his way of driving women mad? She slid the nylon shorts off over her full hips, exposing her thighs.

She lifted his tee shirt, and he quickly pulled it off over his head, exposing fine blond chest hair and sinewy muscles. She outlined his bruises with her fingertip, and bent over and kissed his abdomen where the worst of the bruising remained.

"Does it hurt?" she asked quietly. She looked up at him and he shook his head no.

She rubbed her hands over him, from his waist up his chest, stopping at his shoulders, which she kneaded with her fingers. She saw the longing in his eyes. She kissed him with excruciating softness, barely touching him as her tongue probed his. His breath quickened and a low moan escaped him. He slid his hands under the straps of her leotard, pulling it downward and exposing her breasts and belly, slipping it down her legs to the floor. He pulled her closer and kissed her hard, and she could feel his arousal.

She moved to the middle of his unmade bed. He removed his shorts and joined her, sitting back against the pillows. He pulled her to him, her torso facing him and her legs away as she sat on one hip. He kissed her again as his hand explored her body. He ran his fingers over the smooth skin of her thigh, up her waist to her breast. She moaned as he massaged her nipple with his thumb, ever so lightly, then squeezed it between his fingers. He explored her mouth and face with his kisses, biting her gently, whispering her name, chewing on her earlobe. His hand moved down to her belly and the curls below it, and he combed them with his fingers. She shifted slightly to allow him access to her, moaning at the thought of him touching her there, her arousal so great. His fingers entered her and found her sweet spot. Her head fell back and she closed her eyes as he touched her. He worked her with his hand until he felt her trembling and her breathing quicken, he knew she was coming. He watched her face as she panted and he whispered to her as she hit her peak,

"That's it, come for me beautiful."

Her hand flew to her face as she tried not to make noise.

"I want to hear you," he whispered. "Don't stop your sounds, you've no idea what they're doing to me."

Thea writhed as he continued to fondle her. He was enjoying the view of this wanton creature's abandon at his attentions. She moved his hand away when she could stand it no longer.

"Please!" she gasped. He held her and kneaded her buttock as she caught her breath and tried to regain a modicum of composure. She wanted to repay his exquisite attentions in spades. She whispered to him as she tenderly kissed him.

"How do you want me to make love to you?"

He thought he'd come right then. Most of the women he'd been with in recent years just expected him to take the lead. She was a willing and active participant who wanted to please him, to make love to him, how thrilling!

"Oh, Thea," he growled. "Come here." He pulled her on top of him, and she moved to straddle him. She touched his penis with long, tender strokes. He moaned. Their eyes were locked. She eased herself down on him. His eyes closed as he breathlessly moaned again. She slowly went to work on him, moving in slow circles on him. She felt him adjust his legs to better move into her. She took his hands from her waist, entwined his fingers in hers and pushed his hands up over his head. As she did her motion changed, to a hard up and down movement. He could only think of one way to describe it. She was fucking him and he loved it. Her eyes were all lust. He needed to be on top of her. He overpowered her and flipped her on her back, sliding out of her as they made the transition. He pulled her to him and slid back in, hard.

"Oh, yeah," she moaned. She pulled her legs up so he could get deeper.

They were wild. Her noises made him crazy. She came again and he held her hands down so she couldn't cover her face. He lost control as he watched her, his heavy breathing leading to a long, low growl. Even though he was breathless and wasn't sure he could maintain consciousness, he enfolded her in his arms and kissed her passionately, holding her and stroking her until their breathing slowed.

She studied his face, relaxed with eyes closed, and traced his cheekbone with her finger. It was a strong, handsome face. He was great in bed. She liked him. She loved his kid. Was she falling for him? She tried not to let the fear at that possible realization show in her eyes. Too late, he saw something but misconstrued what it might be.

"Um, I guess it's a bit late to be asking about this."

"About what?"

"Birth control?" he said softly.

"The factory was closed 3 years ago. But thanks for asking, even if it was a bit late." She smiled.

"Did I score high enough for another go?" he asked.

"Right now?" she asked, surprised.

He laughed and raised an eyebrow. "With you I probably could."

"I will take that as a complement."

"As you should."

"You were fabulous. I very much want this to happen again," she said.

"So do I," he whispered lustily as he closed his mouth over hers.

SEVENTEEN

They eventually got up and showered together, Jas realizing what a mistake it was when his soapy hands moved up over her breasts and he immediately was aroused. He ended up making love to her against the wall of the shower, with a satisfactory outcome for both of them. He couldn't remember the last time he'd made love three times in as many hours, and all before coffee.

She sneaked into her room to change and met him up on deck. Young Brian brought coffee and juice, pouring for them both as Jas helped her with her chair.

"Are you ready for your breakfast now, miss?" he asked.

She chuckled, licked her lips as she shook her head knowingly and said "Yeah, I'd say I'm ready for breakfast." Jas burst out laughing and had to look away.

"Brian, I'll have the same," he added.

Brian was grinning and blushing, as he'd asked Charles about bringing the lady breakfast after she and Mr. Collins disappeared three hours ago, and Charles told him there were to be NO interruptions. It didn't take the staff long to figure out what was going on.

Tori and Trevor eventually made their way up on deck, drank some juice and asked where they were. Thea pointed out landmarks on the shore, and told them they were headed to Savannah Bay for some great snorkeling. At least that's where the yacht was headed; snorkeling was up to her father.

"Can we, dad?" Tori asked excitedly?

God, he thought to himself, now I have two women I don't want to disappoint.

"Yes, yes." He smiled as Tori hugged him. He glanced a knowing look at Thea and she smiled. They were going to be discreet and not let Tori know they had become lovers.

The launch took them to shore, navigating between the reefs. The foursome piled out onto the pristine sand. There were two other people on the whole beach. Duncan stayed in the launch a distance from shore while Roy joined the others on the beach, setting up an umbrella and then walking the perimeter to take a look around. Tori pointed to an outcropping of reef above the water.

"Tori, Donny and I snorkeled around there and almost got stranded on top."

"How?" she asked.

"The tide went out and we were in a pool on the far side, and there almost wasn't enough water for us to swim out. You're not supposed to touch the reef, or stand on it, so we would have had to damage it if we couldn't swim out. Plus there's some coral that hurts if you touch it."

"Fire coral, right?" Trevor asked.

"Exactly."

Thea helped Tori with her mask, and they all swam out toward the reef. Thea pointed out some hard to see fish and sea animals. She dove down and picked up a sea cucumber and they all touched it and played with it. She showed Jas a hole in the rock and told him there was probably a Moray Eel in there. He dove down and grabbed an empty lobster carcass on the bottom and waved it in front of the hole. Sure enough, the enormous eel stuck its head out. Jas was laughing to himself when he heard Tori scream underwater.

He broke through the surface and found Thea laughing as Tori and Trevor were gabbing a mile a minute about what they'd just seen. As the kids swam off to seek out more of the ocean's mysteries Jas swam up to Thea.

"Thank you."

"For what?" she asked.

"Suggesting we do this. For being so good with her." He slipped his arms around her.

"I like her. She's a great kid. It's not a chore." She said very decisively.

"Thank you anyway." He kissed her.

"Sir, you are indiscreet!" she said, sounding appalled. Then she took the top of his head and pushed him under as she swam off.

They eventually all dragged themselves on shore. Thea made everyone reapply sunscreen, and Roy opened the cooler for them. Jas was amazed at Thea's ability to put down a Red Stripe, and he told her so. She made them all laugh with her exaggerated Boston accent.

"Roy, get ya ass ovah heah and open me anotha friggin' beah, babe. I'm from Bahstan and we don't wait fa nothin'."

Jas and the kids all laughed. Even Roy was chuckling.

Jas sat on the rug that they'd brought, arms around his knees. Trevor was on his stomach, probably sleeping after the huge sandwich he'd just inhaled. Jas watched Victoria and Thea walking down the beach. They stopped and looked at things they'd pick up, wade into the water, come back out and look some more. It pleased him to see them get on so well. Thea was beautiful in her simple black maillot, with her hair piled up under a cap and her sunglasses on. He watched as they kneeled and dug into the sand, then both jumped up and ran away, laughing and holding each other. He couldn't tell what was going on but it made him laugh. He approached.

"Dad, look!" Tori yelled.

He saw little crabs scurrying all over the beach. He chuckled.

"Is this what the fuss is about?" he asked.

Tori was carrying a bleached out conch shell.

"Let me see your shell," he said. She handed it to him. "Anybody in there, you think?" he looked at Thea.

"No, too dry. How are your lungs?" she asked.

"I don't know, why?" he asked, wide eyed.

"Blow into it. See if you can make it sound the siren."

"You're kidding, right?" he asked. She shook her head. He gave it a go. Halfway though his first attempt they all doubled over in laughter.

"You sound like a goose in heat," Thea cried. "Try again."

He took several minutes to regain his composure, as every time he put his lips to the shell they would all break up. Finally he blew into it hard and at length, and it made a wonderful sound.

"Neptune has arrived," Thea said as she curtsied to him. Tori jumped up and down.

"Dad, we need this on the ship!"

"Yes, we do," he said, smiling.

They made their way back and Trevor asked about lobsters, since this was what the island was famous for. Thea, trying to be her helpful self, mentioned that Smitty would sell them some lobsters if they wanted to cook them on the ship. She would live to regret mentioning Smitty... Jas directed the bridge to stop in Island Harbour so they could take the launch to shore.

"Jas, you don't need to do this! I'm sure we can find lobster in Sandy Ground," she said.

"We're going right by, why not stop?" he asked.

"I'll be happy to go in and get them, then," Thea said.

"And I'll be happy to go with you," he said, smiling.

The launch landed at Smitty's dock, and Thea prayed he was not there. They disembarked and strode toward the entrance. Smitty looked up.

"Oh my God, it be the big white woman!" Smitty cried out excitedly. "Thea, my love!"

Thea couldn't help but laugh.

"Smitty, you rogue, how are you."

He picked her up in a bear hug and spun her around. Jas looked on with an amused grin.

"How are you, beautiful? How is Peter?" Smitty asked. Smitty was a friend of Peter's family, and knew the two had been a couple. He had not seen her for almost a year.

"I'm fine, Smitty. Peter is fine, but we're not together anymore."

Smitty looked flabbergasted. Jas' expression grew serious.

"What did that stupid man do?" Smitty asked, not really expecting an answer. Thea introduced Smitty to Jas. Jas smiled as he shook hands.

"You are a lucky man to be in the company of Miss Thea!" he exclaimed.

"I agree wholeheartedly, sir." Jas replied, looking a tad too serious for Thea's liking. They chatted a bit more, and Thea negotiated a good price on lobsters, after resorting to calling him a thief and scoundrel. Smitty hugged her and wished them all the best as they motored toward The Victoria in the launch.

127

Jas waited until they were back on the yacht to mention the interaction between Thea and Smitty. The teenagers were showering and the chef had taken the lobsters to the galley, and Jas and Thea were alone on deck.

"How do you know Smitty?" he asked, quietly.

"I met him years ago when Kip and his son and I vacationed here. I met him again when I had been on Nevis for a year. He's a friend of the Moses family. I saw him at a holiday party at their house."

"Peter Moses? The police chief?" he asked. She nodded.

"So the Peter he asked you about was Chief Moses?"

"Yes."

"You were a couple?"

"Yes."

"Where you planning on keeping that a secret?" he asked. His face darkened. His demeanor reflected hurt, not anger.

"When was I supposed to mention that?" she asked. "It's not like we've known each other all that long, Jas. I'm sure it would have surfaced eventually."

"When did you last see him?" Good God, she didn't want to answer that. She also didn't want to lie to him.

"When did we break up?" she asked, trying to not have to lie. He turned to face her fully.

"When did you last sleep with him, Thea?" She felt ill. She didn't lie.

"The night you were attacked," she said quietly.

He closed his eyes and his fists clenched. Why hadn't he listened to himself? he thought. Why did he let her in? He should have kept his distance. It wouldn't hurt so much.

"Please let me explain," she said.

"What is there to explain? I don't own you, you're free to do whatever you want," he said coldly. "I guess I should have been more concerned about safe sex."

"Jas, please don't."

Hearing her say his name was bittersweet. She continued when he said nothing. Her voice was barely a whisper. Jas listened carefully, but tried to look aloof.

"Peter and I were a couple for awhile when he returned to Nevis from England. He was the first man I was with after Kip died. It had been two years since I'd been intimate with anyone, and Peter was kind, and a generous lover. He'd been tested for AIDS in London and had always used precautions. I'd been with the same man for 10 years and had been celibate for 2 years after that, so we saw no need to use anything. I don't love Peter. Peter wants children and a home on Nevis. I'm sterile and I know I won't stay in the Caribbean forever. We're friends. He's too busy to find a wife, I wasn't looking for a long term relationship. We slept together once in awhile because it felt good. No strings attached, that was the deal. He was worried about me the night of the attack and he stayed. That's all. I hadn't expected..." She paused.

He looked up at her. "Expected what?"

"You." She shook her head as if to say she didn't know or didn't understand. He turned back toward the water.

"I'm sorry Jas. The last thing I would ever do is hurt you." She left the deck before he turned around, she didn't want him to see her cry.

Thea went below, tears streaming down her cheeks. She showered and changed, determined to put up a good front for Tori's sake. She could always make her excuses, go ashore tomorrow, and fly back to Nevis.

Jas stood on deck looking out over the water toward the lights on shore. Why was he feeling so horrid? She hadn't lied to him. She could have but she didn't. He'd heard her voice crack as she spoke her last words to him. Was she crying? Did this bother her as much as it was killing him? He hadn't asked her about anyone else in her life. He hadn't even considered it! What an idiot he was! Had he really thought this beautiful, sensual woman had no lovers in three years? What had she meant about not expecting him? Was she falling in love with him? He now knew he'd behaved badly. Why did it hurt him so much that she'd been with someone else? Jealousy? What would she do now? Would she stay on board, or go ashore and return to Nevis? The thought of her leaving made him ache with longing for her. He was in love with her. That's why it hurt so much. But it was too soon, how could he be sure? He was sure of one thing, he needed to apologize, and he needed to convince her he cared for her, but he had to make sure he didn't scare her away.

Jas went below, but as he approached Thea's door he heard her showering. He slipped into his room and did the same.

Thea dressed for dinner and went to the observation deck. Charles poured her a drink and seemed to understand her less than gregarious mood, and allowed her to drift out into the air. She took her drink and leaned against the rail looking out at the sliver of moon.

She wasn't sure the drink was a good idea, she'd probably become maudlin and cry at the slightest provocation. Tori found her and told her that dinner was ready. Thea followed her into the dining room, steeling herself against seeing Jas and what she was sure would be an angry face. As they sat Charles came to the table.

"I'm sorry, but Mr. Collins won't be able to join you this evening." Thea was almost relieved to not have to face him. Charles looked at Thea. "He faxed your notes to his project manager, who researched your information and found you're assumptions were on the mark. They went back to World Markets with a lower offer based on their research and there is a high-level conference call happening right now because of it. I'd say their CEO is mad as a hornet. This all just happened within the last 20 minutes. He asked me to pass on his regrets."

"Charles, has the chef begun cooking the lobsters yet? It would be a shame to have them tonight. We should wait 'till tomorrow. I'd be happy with a sandwich, quite frankly."

Thea wasn't hungry at all, and hated the thought of wasting good food. Tori and Tevor agreed. They'd be better for lunch tomorrow when Tori's dad could have them, too.

Charles returned a moment later and told them a cold platter would be up shortly, and the lobsters had received a stay of execution.

Thea picked at a piece of turkey breast as the kids ate voraciously. The exercise today had made them ravenous, and tired. By 10 PM they were drifting down toward their beds. Thea rationalized that the conference call probably did happen, but Jas took the opportunity to stay in his office afterwards, so he wouldn't have to deal with her. She decided she'd leave first thing in the morning. She went below and undressed, and slid between the sheets. Thankfully she was too tired to cry.

Jas was on the phone for three hours. He wasn't in the best mood to begin with, so the mention of lack of good faith and deceptive practices put him right over the edge. His people in New York looked at each other in awe as they listened to him on the speaker phone taking on Victor Sablan, the CEO of World Markets as well as Dick Corcoran, the head of the Union. His people had armed him with their research by fax, which he'd read over before the call. While nothing was decided that night, the upper management at World Markets who Jas was convinced was in bed with the Union knew they were not going to bamboozle J. Collins Ltd. into a deal with which Jas was not happy. It was after midnight when he went to his cabin. Charles has chastised him for, as Charles put it, whatever he'd said or done to Miss Garrett. He'd told Jas that she had been very melancholy and hadn't eaten a thing at dinner. He'd wanted to talk to Thea, but it was too late tonight. Her light was out. He'd secretly hoped he'd find her in his bed, but after his behavior this afternoon he knew it wouldn't happen. He was exhausted, both physically and emotionally. He was out by the time he hit the pillow.

Thea dreamed of being locked in a room. She was crying and she couldn't open the door. She could see the other side, see her father going after her mother, see the truck heading for Kip's car, and see the men attacking Jas. But she couldn't do anything to stop it. She fought with the door and pounded on it with all her might. When it flew open she found herself sitting up in bed, gasping for air. She wondered if she'd screamed this time, as if she hadn't caused enough trouble already. She was shaking, and sweating, even though the cabin was cool. She felt she would suffocate. She grabbed a cotton blanket from the bed and slipped out of her stateroom, quietly making her way up to the heli-pad.

She sat up there and gulped air, afraid she couldn't get enough. When she remembered the dream she started to cry. Why, she thought, why did you open the door, Mom? She tried to tell herself all the things the shrink told her to do at times like these. Why was the dead of night always so bad? She knew it was worse when she was troubled, and she certainly was troubled now. She knew it would be hours until daylight. She couldn't be rational, she had no strength to fight the fear tonight, so she curled up in the blanket and let the sorrow overtake her. She lay there and sobbed.

Jas looked at the clock when he heard the noise. It was 3 AM. Had he heard something, a shout perhaps? Or was he dreaming? He lay still and listened. He heard shuffling next door, in Thea's room. He heard the door. He didn't know what to do. He'd wanted to talk to her. Was she troubled, too? He thought about his conversation with her when they'd first met. She'd confided in him about her parents, and Kip. What were her words? "The middle of the night can be difficult." He felt like a shit, making her feel bad about a relationship that hadn't even begun. And wouldn't if he continued to behave like this. He got up and threw on his drawstring pants. He gently pushed her door open, but she wasn't there. He went up on deck and saw Tim on patrol. Tim pointed his finger up, signaling to the heli-pad. Jas motioned his thanks. He slowly climbed the steps. His heart fell when he saw her wrapped in a blanket in the fetal position, facing away from him, her shoulders shaking with her sobs. He quietly sat on the deck behind her, unsure of what to do or say. He lay down on his side and molded his body to hers, slipping his arm under her head, pulling her close. She tensed. He smoothed her hair with his fingers and kissed her temple as he whispered to her.

"It's alright, Thea. It's me. Go ahead and cry. Let it out. You're safe here."

She wasn't sure if the tears she shed then were of sadness or relief. She eventually quieted, lying in his arms, her head under his chin. He had continued to stroke and to kiss her hair, murmuring quietly that everything would be all right.

"Are you just having one of those difficult nights you told me about?" he asked.

"I'm a mess," she said, speaking barely loud enough for him to hear.

"Physically or emotionally?" he asked.

"Yes," she replied. He laughed softly. He kissed her temple again as he whispered to her.

"Thea. I'm sorry. I had no right to behave as I did earlier."

She turned to face him. He though she was still beautiful, even with puffy, red eyes.

"You're right, you didn't. So why did you?"

It was a legitimate question.

"Jealousy."

"Jealousy is a wasted emotion. If I wanted to be with Peter I'd be there now, not here with you. Don't do it again," she admonished, tears welling up in her eyes. He was amused and a bit taken aback. He wiped the tears with his thumb.

"I won't. Do you want to tell me why you came up here?"

"Nightmare."

"You want to talk about it?" he asked.

"Not really." They were quiet. "Do you want to talk about your conference call?" she asked.

"Absolutely not," he sighed. "I'll tell you it wasn't pleasant and it was very long. And you armed us with some very valuable information."

"Good," she whispered, regaining some of her missing composure.

"Do you think you could go back to sleep?" he asked.

"No."

"Why?"

"I'm hungry," she said. He laughed.

"Charles told me you didn't eat much tonight. Shall I rouse the chef?"

"Don't be ridiculous. Let's just go raid the kitchen," she said.

"The galley," he corrected, smiling.

"Yeah, whatever."

They moved down to the galley, Thea leaving her blanket in a heap by the door. She immediately began to forage, and Jas saw he was in good hands so he sat on the counter and watched. She opened the large refrigerator doors and her nipples stood at attention. He became aroused, and was once again delighted by his immediate reaction to her. Her oversized tee shirt went to her mid thighs, and he was sure she wore nothing beneath it. It had a "Colors of the Caribbean" logo and a Barbados insignia on it. She grabbed several items from the refrigerator and made her way to the stove. She found a frying pan, and began an interesting concoction.

"Did you have dinner?" she asked.

"No."

"You're in for a treat," she joked.

She finished up her delicacies, and hopped up on the counter next to him. She took a corner of what looked like a croque monsieur, and fed it to him.

"Ah, grilled cheese and chutney," he said, smiling. "I grew up eating these."

She smiled back. They mashed the buttery sandwiches into their mouths with abandon. She started to clean up.

"Thea, it's alright. The staff will do it in the morning."

"They didn't make the mess, they shouldn't have to clean it up."

"Is this how you're going to be with the household help?" he asked, half seriously. She turned and looked at him quizzically. What was this about? she thought.

"Oh, I'll just let them all go sit by the pool while I vacuum," she said, joking. He walked over to her and turned her around, and bent over and kissed her. He realized it was too soon for this conversation, and that he'd scare her if he continued.

"Let's go," he said as she put the last of the dishes in the dishwasher.

They got into his bed together, and he pulled her close. She was facing away from him, her head tucked under his chin. His arm was around her and she felt safe. Maybe she could sleep. She listened for his breathing to deepen and steady, but it didn't. And his arm was still pretty tense around her body. He rolled over on his back and sighed. She turned to face him.

"What's wrong?" she asked.

"I can't just lay here in bed with you. I want you too much."

"And that's a problem?" she asked, getting to her knees and taking her oversized tee shirt off over her head. She was on her knees before him, naked, beautiful and with a seductive pout on her gorgeous mouth. He reached up for her and pulled her to him, rolling her on her side. He explored her flesh with his hands. He kissed and fondled her, and she stroked him and cooed the most intimate sounds to him. Her quiet sighs and longing looks were driving him mad. He finally rolled her onto her back and entered her, making her moan with pleasure. He felt as though he was in an altered state. The emotional drain, the lack of sleep, the absolute heat he felt for her and the feeling he now was sure was love had wound him tighter than a top. He made love to her deliciously slowly, knowing he really wanted to fuck her violently and scream with her as they climaxed. He teased her and brought her to the edge, playing with her and finally making her wild with her desire. He watched joyously as he took her over the top. He saw her back arch, felt her nails dig into his flesh as her legs wrapped around him and he kissed her deeply, needing to control her and overtake her as she came. The emotion drove him mad. He followed her into her bliss, crying out as his release overtook him. When he was once again aware of his surroundings she was kissing him and running her fingers through his hair, panting and trying to catch her breath, as was he. He wound his limbs around her and held her close. As they began to drift off he whispered to her.

"I'm falling in love with you, Thea."

Her eyes snapped open. She wasn't sure if she really heard it or not. His breathing sounded like he'd already gone to sleep, but he pulled her closer and kissed her, falling asleep blissfully in her arms.

EIGHTEEN

Sal and Joey had hooked up with Rico, the guy with the boat that the boss had told them about. Rico had a network of buddies in the fishing business that could keep tabs on the goings on in most any harbor in the Caribbean, for a price. These fishermen where on the up and up, they just got paid a bit for information. No laws were broken and everybody was happy. Joey was able to report back that the yacht was in Anguilla, and they were able to keep a close eye on the goings on, being in the harbor themselves and all. That's when they were told that the negotiations with this Collins guy were not going as well as planned and perhaps they needed to re-send the message.

Dick Corcoran hadn't been able to find anything slanderous or scandalous out about Victor Sablan, and realized his best bet was to let the sale go through, take his hush money and disappear. When the offer Collins had on the table decreased so did his percentage, and that wasn't what he had in mind. So the message that needed to be sent to Jasper Collins was that the offer needed to return to the original amount. Once the papers were signed they'd turn his world right side up again.

NINETEEN

Jas slept very late the next day. Thea awoke and slipped out of his room, and had an opportunity to go through her normal routine of yoga, grab a shower and have coffee by herself up on deck before anyone else surfaced. She tried to use yoga as her meditation, to make her mind still, but it was so difficult today. Her mind raced with thoughts about Jas' words before they finally slept last night. She was happy to have some time alone to think. Once again she was drawn to the helipad, her high perch where she would be undisturbed. She sat with her big mug of coffee and looked out over the emerald colored water. He told her he was falling in love with her. What did that mean? A relationship? Continuity? Leaving Nevis? Being the girlfriend of a high-powered multi-millionaire? Going back to the real world? Thea wasn't sure she was ready for any of those things. But why not? She knew she was in love with him, too. But all the things she had loved had been taken away from her. Was she afraid something might happen to Jas and Tori? Maybe. Or was that just a cop out? It was easy to use fear as an excuse when there were other things at issue. If she loved him, and she loved his daughter, and she knew they felt the same about her then what was the problem? She couldn't go straight from Nevis to Jas' house, not that it had been offered, mind you. Her reintroduction into the real world would need to be at her own pace. She had her own money, she'd need to decide what work she would do. When would they see each other? He traveled constantly, although he was home most weekends with Victoria. Where would she live? Maybe she was letting her mind move too fast. Maybe his semi conscious murmuring was not to be taken seriously at all. Perhaps she should just be casual about this because it might just end up being nothing, and in a few days they would go their separate ways. She took a deep breath and just decided to slow down.

She heard footsteps behind her. She turned and looked up to see a very sleepy looking man approaching her with a coffee mug held out. She smiled at him as he sat next to her and she filled his cup from the thermos pot she had brought with her up on deck. His eyes were half-open, and he looked amazingly sexy. She leaned over and kissed him. He nuzzled her neck and then sat up, took a swallow and put the cup down. He reached out and pulled her close to him, maneuvering her so she sat between his legs with her back to his chest. He wrapped his arms around her and kissed her temple.

"I didn't like waking up without you," he said softly. "I reached over and you weren't there."

"I don't think you're awake yet, so I'm not sure that counts." She tried to sound light and casual.

"I believe you're right," he agreed. "But when I do wake up I'd like to talk." Thea's heart raced.

"About?" she asked.

"Us," he replied.

"Jas," she began. He motioned with his hand for her to stop. He was silent for a moment.

"I was serious last night, Thea." It was as though he'd listened to her inner conversation this morning and was responding. "I'm falling in love with you. I haven't felt like this in a very, very long time. It scares me, but this marvelous feeling outweighs my fears."

"Jas, you hardly know me. Why would you want to get involved with someone with all of my emotional baggage?" she asked.

"Don't you think you've dealt with most of it? I think you're healthier emotionally than most people I know. You seem to have risen above it."

"Oh, yeah. I did a great job dealing with it last night. You found me up here in a puddle in case you've forgotten."

He squeezed her tight and kissed her hair.

"None of us is perfect. I'm willing to deal with your baggage," he said. "You'd be getting involved with a ready made family. How would that feel?"

"I think you are moving way too fast. I won't lie to you; I have very strong feelings about you, too. And about Tori. But there's all this... stuff I still need to figure out."

"Define strong feelings," he said.

"What?"

"You heard me. How do you feel about me?" he asked. She paused before answering.

"Terrified."

"What? Why?"

Thea started to tremble. Jas felt it and turned her around so he could look into her eyes. Thea saw he was wide-awake now. He studied her face. His intensity was melting her. He took her shoulders and gently squeezed them as he spoke.

"Why do I terrify you?" he asked again, searching her face and then looking deep into her eyes. She hesitated.

"Because you're so damned easy to love," she whispered. The intensity of his look remained, but his face lightened, as though a weight had been removed from his shoulders.

"Do you?" he asked. He wanted to hear her say it. He wanted to know if her feelings for him were the same.

"It scares me to say this to you so soon. This is all happening so fast."

"Thea, tell me how you feel about me." His look was dead serious.

"I'm in love with you," she said very quietly as she looked down. He took her chin and gently made her look at him.

"Tell me again."

"And I love you." She looked straight at him as she spoke and saw the joy in his eyes at her words. He bent and kissed her gently. When he pulled back he smiled ever so slightly before he spoke.

"I love you, too."

TWENTY

Thea and Jas spent a casual day in each other's company. Trevor and Tori sat in deck chairs and listened to each other's CDs, played games and swam off the bow of the yacht. Thea had taken photos all the time during the trip. She had caught them swimming and snorkeling the day before, at dinner the first evening and even having the lobsters for lunch. They all discussed what they might do later that evening. Thea mentioned Johnno's.

"What is Johnno's?" Tori asked. Thea pointed it out on the beach.

"It's a place the local bands come to play music. It's great! There's a mix of tourists and locals, and everybody dances. It is really a fun time."

"Dad, can we go?" Tori asked. Jas smiled and looked at Thea.

"The kids aren't too young?" he asked with a wink.

"Da-a-ad!!" Tori chided.

"No, there are little kids there early in the evening. They serve food until the bands start." Thea said, smiling at his teasing of his daughter.

"Sounds good. Lets do it."

Tori smiled broadly. "Great! Thanks Dad!"

Chef prepared a light meal for them and they took the launch to Sandy Ground at around 9 PM. Tim and Duncan accompanied them, and stood near the doors as the foursome entered the open structure and made their way to the bar. Duncan came close to Jas and whispered in his ear.

"Sir, we're going to have a rough time keeping an eye on things here. It's very open. If you don't all stay together and someone tries to get at you we could have a problem."

"We'll stay together. Just stick close. Everything will be fine," Jas told him with a positive nod of the head. Duncan nodded back and moved toward Tim. Thea looked at Jas questioningly as she handed him and Tevor each a Caribe beer. Jas motioned for them all to come closer. Tori grabbed her coke and moved nearer to her father. The place was already getting crowded and loud. Jas spoke loud enough for them all to hear.

"Duncan and Tim are worried about the crowd and the open access to us. Lets just try to stay together as much as possible, and stay within Tim and Duncan's fields of vision. Alright?" Everyone nodded.

Tori looked around suspiciously. Jas hated making her feel uncomfortable. He wanted so much to make her upbringing as normal as possible. Thea saw his look of concern. She slipped her arm around Tori.

"Just think about telling your grandchildren of your great Caribbean adventures!" she said enthusiastically. Tori laughed, and Jas' twinkling eyes smiled at her. The music started up, loud and funky, and a young Anguillan man asked Tori to dance. She looked at her father, who eyed the young man. He smiled and nodded and the two of them danced nearby. Jas took Thea's beer and handed both his and Thea's to Trevor, pulling her out onto the floor. They danced near Tori and stayed in eyeshot of the two burly bodyguards.

The music was hot, the dancing didn't stop and the beer flowed all night. They were having a great time, all laughing and drinking, and enjoying each other. When Thea could stand it no longer she told Jas "If I don't get to the ladies I'm going to explode. Beer isn't something you buy, it's something you rent!"

Jas laughed. Tori heard her and piped up that she needed to go, too. Duncan accompanied the two ladies to the facilities around the backside of the bar. Trevor asked his uncle if he could have a word, and the two of them made their way to the far end of the bar where the noise was just above a dull roar. Tim watched them from his position by the door. Trevor began speaking about his possible career paths. The beer relaxed him enough to feel he could talk freely with his uncle.

"You know, I'm attending university this year, and I need to decide what I'm going to do with my life. I'm really confused." Jas could see the young man was troubled. He let Trevor pontificate about his options, asking questions to make sure he understood what his nephew was thinking. They were deep in conversation and had lost track of the time the ladies had been gone.

Tori and Thea giggled as they entered the ladies room. It really wasn't someplace you wanted to spend a great deal of time in.

"Tori, honey, I think you definitely want to hover above the seat in here," Thea said, chuckling. Tori was giggling and holding onto the wall.

"If you keep that up I'm going to piss myself!" Tori replied. They both laughed as they read the graffiti in the stalls. Tori exited her stall first and Thea could here the water running at the sink. When it got quiet Thea called her name.

"Tori? Wait for me!" Thea got to the sink to wash her hands and looked around for a mirror to fix her lipstick. There wasn't one. She grabbed a paper towel and felt someone smash something into her face. She struggled, hitting at the person's arms that were holding her, but the strong, sweet smell on the rag at her face was making her dizzy and sick to her stomach. She remembered the smell. Ether? She flashed back to her childhood tonsillectomy, and saw operating room lights on the ceiling just before she lost consciousness.

TWENTY ONE

Jas looked at his watch and looked up at Trevor with a questioning look.

"Haven't they been gone a particularly long time, even for women?" he asked. Trevor chuckled and nodded his agreement. The two of them approached Tim, and Jas voiced his concern. The three men walked around the outside of the bar where a small crowd was gathered by the restrooms. The sight of the gathering caused them to move faster and Tim pushed his way through to find Duncan on the ground with blood on the back of his head. He was trying to rise and a policeman was attempting to assist him.

"What in bloody hell happened?" Tim screamed at Duncan and the policeman. Trevor was stunned. Jas became almost frantic.

"Victoria! Thea!" he screamed as he ran into the women's restroom. It was empty. The trashcan had been tipped over and the towel holder was knocked onto the floor. Whoever had been in here had struggled. He ran back out.

"They're gone. Did anyone see anything?" he asked of the crowd. "My daughter and my friend have been abducted. Did anyone see anything?" he screamed. The policeman approached and Jas saw Tim and Trevor holding Duncan up.

"Sir, I was called over by this man, who thought your friend on the ground was drunk."

The cop pointed to a young black man standing nearby, and motioned him over.

"Sir, we need to get you back to the yacht where you'll be safe," Tim said to Jas.

"I'm not going anywhere," Jas barked. Tim backed down knowing the boss was as serious as a heart attack. Jas spoke to the young man with the cop.

"Please, this is very important. Tell me what you saw."

The young man shifted from foot to foot. The officer interrupted before he could speak.

"Sir, why do you think your daughter and friend were abducted? Why would someone want to do that?" he asked.

Jas explained the attack on Nevis, and how the issue he was being warned about had heated up recently.

"Ah," the officer began, "you are Jasper Collins."

"How would you know that?" Jas asked, looking troubled.

"Because Peter Moses called us to tell us a friend of his was staying with you on your yacht, and he was afraid she might be in danger should someone want to harm you. We have been watching for your launch and trying to keep an eye on things, unofficially. I'm afraid we did not see you come ashore tonight."

Jas was angry and frustrated and jealous all at once. He understood Peter's depth of feeling for Thea and it made him crazy. Yet Peter's intentions hadn't saved her.

"Well, the woman with my daughter was Peter's friend. They would have taken her as well as my daughter to get to me. Can we please try to find them?" His voice rose as he spoke. The young man finally said something.

"I saw a bloke helping a really drunk woman to a car, and they sped off. Then I came around the corner to use the john, and I tripped over him," he said, pointing to Duncan. "I thought he was drunk, too. I called for the police." The young man seemed uncomfortable.

"What did the woman look like? Did you see a young girl with her?" Jas asked.

"The woman had red hair. I didn't see a girl, but there were others in the car."

"What kind of car?" the policeman asked.

"A white or tan 4-door. I don't know what type. It had a dent in the rear fender."

The cop had radioed for assistance and was joined by another officer very quickly. He requested the new cop question all those standing around, and had the band make an announcement that they needed any information anyone might have. He took Duncan, Tim, Trevor and Jas to the police station, where an EMT tended Duncan's head. The police chief was summoned and he got the story quickly from his officer and Jas. He dispatched his remaining vehicle out to look for the car the young man had seen, and called his off duty officers for assistance in their personal cars. He called several local fishermen as well as the marina managers to keep an eye on the anchorages. He had the dispatcher call the rental car agencies and ask about a vehicle fitting the description. While he did this Jas called the marine operator and was patched through to the Victoria.

He gave Charles his instructions.

TWENTY TWO

Peter had been having a drink with Sam and Irene at the Figtree Inn while he waited for Jett to finish up for the evening. Jett's tire was flat and the spare had gone missing, so Peter agreed to drive him home that night. Peter's beeper went off just as Jett joined them in the great room. Sam offered the phone in the office and Peter disappeared around the corner. Irene was discussing the next day's menu with Jett, and offering to pick him up in the early afternoon in case his car wasn't repaired by then. Peter came back looking furious.

"Peter, is everything alright?" Irene asked.

"Thea and Victoria Collins have been abducted," he said, his voice shaking. Irene's hands flew to her face. Sam's jaw dropped open. Jett spoke.

"What's happened and what are you going to do?" His voice was even and quiet, but the young man's hands were clenched into fists.

"Jasper Collins' helicopter is at the Nevis airstrip. His assistant is beeping the pilot, who I will meet there in 20 minutes. He will fly me to Anguilla to assist in the investigation. I'll need to stop by the station to pick up the file on the two men Thea photographed. I just hope." He stopped.

"That they don't recognize her!" Irene wailed, tears streaming. Sam pulled his wife to him and tried to comfort her.

"I'm going with you," Jett said. Peter looked at him but said nothing for a moment. Then he nodded.

"Don't worry about anything here, Jett. We'll get Lovey to come out of retirement for a couple of days," Irene said through her tears. Jett kissed her cheek. Irene hugged Jett and Peter in turn. "Bring her back quickly.

We'll be praying for them," Irene whispered as the brothers left the Inn.

"Call us! Let us know what's happening!" Sam yelled as they jogged toward Peter's jeep.

TWENTY THREE

Jas knew that Peter Moses would do everything in his power to get Thea, and therefor Victoria, out of harm's way. He hated that he was using Peter, but his love for his daughter and his deepening feelings for Thea overrode any guilt his conscience could manifest. Thea had told him she didn't love Peter, but they'd had a relationship and it might still be going on if she hadn't met Jas. Relationships weren't as simple as Thea made them out to be, he thought. If she'd continued to sleep with Peter perhaps her feelings for him might have deepened. What was he thinking this for? His baby was missing! As well as the woman he loved. Get them back and worry about the other stuff later, he thought.

Jas had instructed Charles to contact the US offices of J. Collins, Ltd. and inform the legal departments as to what happened. They could contact the appropriate agencies regarding ransoms negotiation, and wait for the call from the kidnappers. The PR agency could get to work on necessary public statements so whoever was behind this would not have the upper hand from a publicity standpoint. Even putting all the wheels over which he had control into motion Jas felt as helpless as a rowboat in a tidal wave.

TWENTY FOUR

Thea came to with a terrible ache over her left eye. Her shoulder was sore, and she quickly realized it was from the awkward position she'd been lying in. She tried to right herself and realized her hands were tied behind her and her ankles were bound. She began to shake violently from a mixture of fear and rage. She looked around and tried to get her bearings. They were in a room made of cinderblock, which was not uncommon in the Caribbean. This room was unfinished, and had dirt floors and a corrugated tin roof. A garage or a shed, perhaps? Where was Tori? Had they taken her, too, or had she gotten away? Thea started to cry from frustration. She finally righted herself and the pain in her shoulder subsided a bit. She'd been treated roughly, her ankle hurt, her bare legs were scraped and her clothes were dirty. She looked around some more. Off to the side and slightly behind her she could see what might be a body. Oh, Dear God please let her be alive! Thea inched her way over and pushed at what she could now see were Tori's legs.

"Tori!" she whispered, "Tori, honey, wake up!" Thea's voice cracked as she spoke. She'd never felt this kind of fear. "Tori, please!"

Thea saw the young woman stir. She sighed with relief in knowing she was at least alive. Tori's head rose slightly. She too was tied up.

"What happened? Where are we? Why does my head hurt like this?" she asked.

"Shh, quiet. Not too loud, OK? I don't know who's around."

"Why are we here?" Tori asked, but the realization struck as she spoke and Thea could hear the fear in her voice.

"Tori, your head hurts from the stuff they used to knock you out. It'll go away."

"We've been kidnapped, haven't we?" she sobbed.

"Yes."

"Aren't you scared?"

"Yes, honey, I am. But I know your father is doing everything he can to find us. I just know it. And we have to have faith in him, OK?" She tried desperately to sound confident for Tori's sake but felt she'd failed.

"Thea, what are we going to do?" Thea could hear the horror in Tori's voice.

"Ok, Ok, um... The first thing is we're going to stay alive. When the men who did this come in, don't look at them. Look away and close your eyes. I don't want them to think we can identify them."

"Are they the same sods who attacked my father?" Tori asked.

"Probably," Thea replied.

"But you took pictures of them, didn't you?" Tori asked.

"Yes, but they don't know that." Thea whispered.

"OK."

"Now, I'm going to try to stand up and see if I can figure out where we are." Thea attempted to roll onto her knees, but with her hands tied behind her she couldn't balance and kept falling back.

"Tori, I'm going to move over to you and sit with my back against yours. If we push toward each other at the same time we can stand up, OK?" Thea said, still shaking.

"Alright."

They sat back to back and pushed together as they walked themselves upright. Thea's ankle was on fire but she fought through it. Once standing she realized her ankle couldn't take any weight. She hobbled over to a high window, trying not to cry out in pain. She could barely see out of it, but she could see the ocean and it was calm. They must be on the Caribbean side of the island, in a protected cove. There didn't seem to be anything else around, and she couldn't hear anyone. She looked at Victoria who was trembling from fear, as it was easily 80 degrees in the small room. She winced as she stumbled toward the door that must have had a bolt across the outside, as the doorknob turned freely and she could move it toward her a bit. She made her way back toward Tori, her ankle now throbbing even worse.

"Turn around. I want to see how they tied the ropes. I want to see if I can untie you." The girl moved around. "Tori, does anything else hurt? Do you think you're injured?"

"No, I don't think so. I'm just really scared."

"I know."

They heard a car pulling up to the shed.

"Sit down here. Slide down the wall. Bury your face in my shoulder and DON'T LOOK AT THEM." Thea whispered urgently. They landed in a heap at the base of the wall and Tori hid her face from view. Then she began to cry. Thea couldn't remember ever being this afraid in her life. What she'd gone through with her parents made her grief stricken and angry, but fear like this had never gripped her before.

"It's OK, it'll be fine. Just be calm." Thea whispered, as much to convince herself as to convince Tori. They heard voices and a key in the lock, and the door clattered open. Thea kept her head bowed and looked at the ground.

"Well, look who woke up?" A man with a New Jersey accent said sarcastically. Thea and Tori remained silent. "Ladies, let me welcome you to your home away from home. Not as nice as the yacht, but it'll have to do until we can get what we want from the kid's old man."

Another man walked in and stood over the women. When he spoke he mumbled badly and Thea could hardly understand him.

"Joey, how come the kid's hidin' her face?" he asked.

"Because she doesn't want to be able to identify us. Red here musta told her not to look. Smart cookie. Though I wouldn't mind lookin' Red in the face, slippin' my tongue in her mouth and havin' a piece a that." His lecherous remark scared Thea and made her sick to her stomach. She wished Tori hadn't had to hear it, and didn't expect Tori's violent reaction.

"You bloody sod. I wish she'd kicked you in the balls instead of the back the night you attacked my father." She said it with her face hidden, but they heard her. Thea winced. Tori was crying, not aware of what she'd just done. The first man spoke.

"You! It was you that ruptured my goddamn kidneys? You bitch!" he spat as he raised his arm and slapped her with the back of his hand. She didn't see it coming with her head down and he connected with her right cheek. She had no free hands to balance and the blow sent her sideways, crashing on top of Tori. Tori screamed.

"Don't look at them," Thea mumbled through her aching jaw.

"I deserve to fuck her for what she did to me." The other man stepped in front of him.

"Get outta here. It's bad enough we kidnapped her and she ain't even the one we need. I ain't gettin involved in no rape charge."

Thea saw the first man's legs as he walked out. Tori was sobbing. The second man spoke.

"You're gonna be here awhile so ya better make the best of it. There'll be someone outside the door all night. We'll be back to bring you food and let you use the toilet."

"If there's going to be a guard, do we have to be tied up?" Thea asked.

"Yeah, it's better that way. We don't take no chances."

"Look, I think my ankle's broken. Can you at least loosen the rope?"

"Sorry about the ankle. It got stuck in the car door." He sounded genuinely apologetic.

The thought of her ankle being smashed by a car door was not an image Thea wanted to keep. He bent and loosened the knot, and retied it less tightly. Thea watched how he'd tied it hoping she could untie Tori.

"I'll bring some ice and bandages in the morning," he mumbled.

"Thanks for..." Thea didn't know how to say it. Thanks for not letting him rape me? She still hadn't looked at him.

"Yeah." He said. He got up and walked out, bolting the door behind him.

Tori was a mess.

"Thea, what did I do? I'm so sorry." She was sobbing and looked so miserable. Thea wanted to hold her and comfort her but her damned hands were bound. Words would have to suffice.

"Tori, it's alright. He didn't hurt me, there's no damage done. They're gone for now. Really, honey. I'm OK." In spite of herself tears of frustration trickled down her cheeks.

"I bollixed up so badly. You must hate me." Tori looked so forlorn.

"Don't be ridiculous. I love you. Now stop it."

"You love me?" Tori asked quietly.

"Of course I do you ninny," Thea whispered, smiling. She leaned over and kissed her forehead. Tori rested her head on Thea's shoulder.

"What are we going to do?" Tori asked, sounding defeated.

"If there's a guard outside I want to see him. I want to know what we're up against." Thea whispered. "And I don't know where we are, so I need to wait till daylight to get my bearings. I'll untie you, 'cause I can tie you up again before they come back, but if you can't get the knots right on me and they find one of us untied it'll make it worse, so I stay tied up and tonight we just wait."

Thea proceeded to maneuver her arms down and under her backside, pulling her legs through so her arms were now in front of her, and in a much more comfortable position. She wrenched her shoulder doing it, though, but at least all that Yoga was good for something. Thea then untied Tori but kept the ropes at the ready to slip onto her wrists should someone return.

"That feels better," Tori said.

"Do you think you can sleep?" Thea asked.

"I don't know. Is your ankle really broken?"

"Maybe. Sprained at least. It feels pretty bad. Scootch down and lay your head on my lap and see if you can get some sleep."

"What about you?" Tori asked.

"I'll be ok."

Tori moved over and got as comfortable as she could on Thea's lap. Thea rubbed her hair and spoke quietly to her, telling her everything was going to be fine. Eventually she heard the steady rhythm of Tori's breathing and knew she was asleep. Thea thought about how frantic Jas must be about Tori's abduction. She wondered if he was worried about her, too. Had Peter been notified? What were they doing to find her and Tori? She hoped they were working fast, for she didn't know how long her captor could save her from his lecherous partner. While she could plan to possibly get Victoria out, Thea knew she couldn't run on this ankle and would have to remain behind.

TWENTY FIVE

Peter and Jett met the helicopter pilot at the Nevis airstrip and were flown to the police station in Anguilla. Jas Collins was with Charles Marston, Trevor, Duncan and Tim in Chief Wilson Cooper's office. Peter knew the chief there, and introduced Jett to everyone. The interchange between Peter and Jas was tension filled.

"Peter, thank you for coming," Jas said to him, "I can't tell you how much I appreciate your help."

"Quite frankly I am here because of Thea and your daughter. And I must add that I cautioned Thea not to join you, so this situation does not please me at all." Peter was obviously annoyed. The two men stared at each other for a moment. Jas nodded to him, signaling he understood and it was obvious to everyone a truce had been called for the sake of the ladies.

The two brothers were quickly brought up to speed on the situation. Peter grilled the bodyguards, Charles, Trevor and Jas about everything that had happened since their arrival on Anguilla, to try to get a sense of anything suspicious that might have occurred. Finally, when Peter was getting annoyed with how little information any of them seemed to have, Jett interrupted.

"Where is Thea's camera?" he asked.

"What?" Jas replied.

"Perfect. Good show, Jett," Peter lit up at this possibility. "Did Thea have her camera with her tonight?"

"No," Jas replied. "She said before we left the yacht that she just wanted to dance tonight and was taking a break from picture taking. She left it in her cabin."

"Good. Get it. Immediately," Peter said urgently.

Charles contacted the ship and the helicopter was dispatched to retrieve the camera bag.

"Thea photographs everything. She may have unwittingly taken some shots of our kidnappers, or at least their vehicle or other transport. We need to get her film developed immediately," Peter said.

Chief Cooper woke the only person on the island with a photo lab and told him to get to his shop. While they waited the men discussed places the women might be being held. Peter's biggest fear was that they'd been removed from the island, as they could be anywhere by now if they had.

"Let's hope they are still on Anguilla," he began. "I think from the M.O. of the two men that attacked you that they do not wish to harm them, but only to terrorize you into doing what they want. They are probably being hidden here somewhere, where they can easily be returned."

Chief Cooper showed them all a map of the island, and pointed out some places where he knew of out buildings that were little used and off the beaten path. It was decided that those places would be searched. In order to know about those places the kidnappers would have had to be helped by a local, and speculation to whom that might be ensued.

"Peter, what do you know of the men we've been investigating as part of the anti-drug initiative? Any movement we can trace to Anguilla?" Chief Cooper asked.

"When I stopped by the station on my way to the airstrip I asked the dispatcher to contact all the tip sources first thing in the morning and get updates." Peter replied.

"Why wait until morning?" Jas asked. "This is an emergency." His tone was even but Peter could sense Jas' sense of urgency.

"Because I don't want anyone to think we're asking these questions as any more than a routine inquiry. If we start waking people in the middle of the night the word will go round that we're looking for someone. It could panic the person we're searching for, and a panicky criminal is more dangerous to Thea and your daughter."

Jas nodded his understanding. The phone rang and two lines lit up simultaneously. The first was the ship saying the pilot was on his way back to the station and to have some one ready to take him to the photo lab with Thea's camera. The second was the New York office of J. Collins Ltd. with the first contact from the kidnappers. Jas' lawyer was on the line.

"Martin I have you on the speaker phone," Jas began. "Chiefs of Police Peter Moses and Wilson Cooper, Jett Moses, Charles, my nephew Trevor and Duncan are in the room with me."

"Gentlemen," Martin Kentwell said in acknowledgement. "We've had a message from a party that chose to remain nameless stating the demands for the release of Victoria. They also mentioned there was a woman with her. Jas, who is she?"

"Martin, her name is Thea Garrett. She is... a friend of mine who was on holiday with us." The emotion in Jas voice caused everyone to sense that this was no casual friendship. Peter tensed.

"They claim that their interests lie in the outcome of the World Markets offer. They want you to honor the original amount that was put on the table prior to your conversation with Sablan and Corcoran earlier this week. Once the agreement is signed, the ink dries and the money is in the bank they'll return Victoria and Ms. Garrett. They also stated any police or FBI involvement and things would get," Martin paused, "um, uncomfortable for them."

Jas' jaw clenched and he visibly paled. He began to shake with rage. Charles Marston spoke.

"Did you contact Sablan?" he asked.

"Of course. And he claimed to know nothing about it. He was apologetic and passed on his concern for the women. He sounded shaken up, like he really didn't know. Or maybe didn't think it would really come about."

"How do you mean?" Jas asked. He knew Victor Sablan to be an upstanding businessman, and wondered who might be pulling the strings.

"Well the big issue with World Markets has always been the union. You know what a tough and dangerous bunch of bastards those guys can be. Since Corcoran got involved in the process early on we've had issues, your attack, for instance. Charles told us about it Jas, so we've been doing some investigating on our own. Chief Moses was kind enough to fax the information he had on the attackers to us."

Jas looked to Peter questioningly.

"Your lawyer stated that you might possibly press charges. I did nothing unusual. You might want to communicate with your lawyer more often," Peter said in a caustic manner.

The lawyer continued.

"The men who attacked you, Joey Landolfi and Tony 'Sal' Salveti, have done union 'work' for years. We're trying to track down Corcoran to see what he has to say. Sablan probably didn't think Corcoran would go to this extreme."

"Can the agreement be upheld legally if Jas signs it just to get Victoria and Thea released?" Charles asked.

"Is it that simple?" Peter interjected. "Won't you have FTC issues and other things that could take weeks or months to reconcile prior to money changing hands?"

"Usually, yes," Martin said. "But this negotiation has been ongoing for some time. The feds have already given their blessing. This could be as little as a two-week timeframe we're looking at if Jas agreed to this today. The analysts would have a field day with a deal going down that quickly. They'd know something was up, but it would be purely speculation. If you fight it after the fact, Jas, the fact remains that they still have your money."

"I don't care about the money," Jas replied.

"Two weeks is a long time," Jett said quietly.

"Martin, we'll ring you back shortly. Ring us up if you get anywhere with Corcoran," Charles said.

The line disconnected. Jas looked at Peter.

"I'm going to tell them yes to the deal and get the wheels in motion. When the deal closes we get Victoria and Thea back. I'll push them to make it happen as fast as possible," Jas said quietly.

"I agree with your decision," Peter began, "but only because it will give the kidnappers a false sense of security. They'll think they've won and perhaps become lax in their duties. If they slip up it may give us a better chance of finding them. Don't get me wrong, I really don't care about your money. They are criminals and what they're doing is illegal. I want them stopped, and I want Thea and Victoria back safely. And I want them back now, not in two weeks."

"But if we can't find them, we at least have the hope they'll be returned after the deal is finalized," Jas added. Peter nodded.

"Hope is all it is though, I'm afraid. Don't delude yourself. Kidnap victim survival rate declines with each day they're held." Peter's gaze never left Jas' face. Jas knew Peter held him responsible for Thea's abduction.

"Then let's get to work trying to find them," Chief Cooper added.

Charles called Martin Kentwell and told him to proceed with the original deal for World Markets.

TWENTY SIX

Thea dozed a bit off and on that night. She was afraid to sleep for fear of the kidnappers coming back to find Tori untied, and even more afraid of her dreams. She tried to stay awake but luckily when she did nod off she did not dream. At first light she woke Tori. The sleepy young woman seemed to not know where she was. When she realized her nightmare had not remained part of the darkness and was really happening, she again looked stricken.

"Tori, I need to tie you up now," Thea said gently. Tori looked scared again. She turned around and put her wrists together. Thea did her best to make it look like the original job. She then forced her legs back through her arms and sat against the wall with her arms behind her, just as the men had left them the night before. They talked quietly and it seemed like forever before they heard a car outside the shack. Thea's stomach knotted as she heard the voice of her sadistic admirer. She whispered to Tori again to not look at them. They heard a key in a padlock and the door was flung open. The sound of it banging off the wall made them jump.

"Mornin' ladies," Joey said with his usual dose of sarcasm. "Did you sleep well?" he went on, not expecting an answer. "Here's the deal. I'm going to untie one of you and bring you out back to use the facilities. Then I'm going to give you some food, and tie you back up again. Capisce? Good. Who wants to go first?"

"Go ahead, Tori," Thea said. "Just keep your head down," she whispered.

"Yeah, you don't wanna look at the bogeyman!" Joey smirked. He untied her ankles and then stood behind her and pulled Tori up by the arms. He freed her wrists and roughly turned her toward the door. Thea was afraid of letting Tori out of her site, especially with that monster. Sal approached Thea with a bag.

"I brought you some ice and an ace bandage. I'll untie ya so you can wrap your ankle up."

He freed Thea and she gratefully stretched her arms and rubbed her wrists. The pressure she'd had to put on them to bring her legs through them made deep marks in her skin.

"I knew he tied you too tight," Sal said to her, looking at her wrists. She was glad he didn't suspect anything else. Thea took the bag of ice and smashed it against the wall to break up the chunks. She placed the whole bag on her throbbing ankle and winced with pain as the cold hit her skin. Uncontrolled tears flowed down her cheeks. She knew the ice wouldn't last long in the heat. She wrapped the ace bandage as tightly as she could, and tried to stand on the ankle. It was excruciating. Joey pushed Tori back into the shed. Thea was happy to see the girl still had her head down. She sat cross-legged on the floor and Sal handed her a sandwich and a bottle of Coke. Joey grabbed Thea's arm and began to drag her out of the door. She tried not to but ended up crying out in pain. He looked down at the wrapped ankle and smiled.

"Gee, I guess I'll just have to carry you," he said, sneering. He picked Thea up before she could move away and trapping her arms to her sides, hoisted her over his shoulder. As he exited the door and rounded the building he slid his hand down to her thigh and massaged it, moving up toward the cheek of her ass. She tensed.

"Oh, yeah, baby. I'd really like a piece a this," he said. She started to squirm, hoping he'd lose his balance and have to put her down. Instead he pushed her up against the side of the building and pinned her to it, holding her arms. "Don't fight me, baby. It'll only be worse," he said as he tried to kiss her. She turned her head and his lips landed on her neck. He kissed her throat and started moving his mouth lower while rubbing his pelvis against hers. She thought she would vomit.

"Please don't do this," she screamed. She began to cry silently as his hand moved to her crotch. Just then Sal appeared behind them.

"Joey, you stupid mother fucker, what did I tell you?" Sal pulled him off of Thea. "I ain't goin down for no rape. Keep away from her."

"You wouldn't be the one doin' the raping, so what's it to you? You want her for yourself? Is that it?"

"Didn't your old man teach you nothin? You wanna pay for it, it's one thing. But you don't never take it against their will. Capisce?" Sal slapped him on the side of the head. Joey lost his mind.

"You don't never touch me, you fuckin asshole. Who the fuck do you think you are? You ain't my boss, here. We both work for Corcoran, just the same we are, both of us. You ever lay a hand on me again I'll break you fuckin' legs, you understand?"

"You touch her again and I'll cut off your dick and make you swallow it, you understand?" Sal spat back at him. Thea wasn't sure she'd heard it right, with Sal still mumbling through his broken jaw, but obviously Joey heard the same thing. He punched Sal in the gut, doubling him over. As he went to land another punch Sal reached up and grabbed him by the balls. The ensuing scream nearly drowned out the sound of the car starting up in the front of the shed. By the time the two men realized something was very wrong it was too late. They knew they couldn't leave Thea, now unbound, by herself in the back of the shed. Sal picked her up to keep Joey away from her and Thea made her weight as dead as possible to make it as difficult as possible for him. Joey could barely stand up and had to creep around the building hanging on to the wall. Thea was hoping against hope that Tori had made a run for it and could get away before one of them could stop her. As they rounded the corner they saw their sentry sprawled across the doorway with an empty Coke bottle next to him. The tan sedan with the dented fender was roaring down the dirt road. Sal dropped Thea in a heap and went running after it at full speed.

Tori looked in the rear view mirror and saw the man running. She was terrified. She'd only driven a car once before, she didn't know where she was going, and she didn't want to leave Thea behind but she knew she needed to get help. She could see another road coming up and she'd have to go left or right. It, too was dirt. What if she went the wrong way and it just ended? They'd catch her. Oh, God, she thought, please let me go the right way. She slowed down to take the turn and the man got closer. She almost lost control of the car. She was so confused by trying to watch behind her and in front, and the brakes were so sensitive! She just managed to make the turn as the man caught up to her and grabbed at the door handle. She screamed and wanted to let go of the wheel and cover her face and hide. She was so scared! She put her foot full on the gas, sending dirt flying behind her. She heard a thump as the man let go and fell. She saw another road ahead, this one tarmac, and two cars went by. Her heart was pounding out of her chest. She made the turn better this time and the tires squealed as she hit the gas and sped away.

TWENTY SEVEN

The man at the photo lab developed all of the rolls in Thea's camera case as well as what was in her camera. He then made enlargements of all of them, as big as he could without losing the sharpness. He handed them off to the helicopter pilot, who caught a nap in the man's office while he waited.

It was 6 AM and the men at the police station had not slept, had eaten little and drunk too much coffee. Tempers were flaring over what to do next. The photographs gave them a much needed focal point. Jett and Trevor taped them all up on the conference room walls. Peter looked around at what looked like a fun filled holiday, with smiling faces enjoying the sun and sand of the Caribbean. Several of the photos made his heart sink. There were a series of beautiful shots that Thea must have set her tripod up to take. She and Jas were holding hands and playfully posing for the lens on the deck of the yacht. He could see her holding the mechanism to trigger the shutter. It was obvious from these photos and the way they looked at each other in them that Thea and Jas had feelings for each other. Peter wanted to take them down, they were painful for him to look at, but they were the ones that had things in the background that might be helpful. They were also the only photos of Thea. Jas was unsure what they were looking for. Chief Cooper and Peter studied each of them carefully taking down any that had no useful background. Wilson Cooper explained to the others that they wanted to study the people, boats, cars and anything else in the photo that might be telling. Peter found something.

"Wilson, look here," Peter began. "Isn't that Rico Costa's boat?"

"Let me get my magnifier." He came back with a large square magnifying glass and held it up to the picture. "Yes. It's his, the 'Rico Suave'."

"Self important little tosser," Peter muttered.

"Be thankful he thinks so highly of himself, Peter," Wilson said, "he could have named it something less memorable, or not named it at all!"

Peter agreed. The phone rang, and the dispatcher entered and motioned for Peter to pick up. Peter acknowledged one of his Nevisian officers on the line, and listened intently. Peter's only comment was "Oh, really?" He thanked the officer and rang off.

The same fishermen who were paid by Rico Costa for information were also paid by the police, or more specifically, the Caribbean Anti-Drug Initiative. The 'soon come' attitude of the Caribbean made it unlikely that any of these fishermen would report to anyone about anything unless probed for information, but Peter's men's inquiries had returned some very useful information.

"Rico requested information from the fishermen earlier this week on the travel path of The Victoria." Peter told the group. Jas' shoulders sagged. He looked defeated.

"We've found our insider," Wilson added. "I'll call the harbor master and the marinas and see if we can locate his boat."

TWENTY EIGHT

When Thea saw a limping Sal making his way down the road her heart leapt with hope that Tori had escaped from her captors. Thea then felt a cold stab of fear at what they might do to her in Tori's absence or because of her escape. She remained balanced against the wall of the shed where Joey had pushed her after Sal had run after the car.

He stood bent over in the doorway waiting for Sal, trying to revive their watchman. Thea was glad glass bottles were still prevalent in the Caribbean, though Tori must have really whacked the guy to knock him out with such a small Coke. Looking at all the roaches on the ground then made Thea think the guy must have been so stoned a tap would have put him under. Joey had choice words for the guy when he finally came around. He looked up to see Sal approaching.

"She got away," Sal said, panting.

"Fuck! The fucking boss is gonna have our heads!" Joey shouted.

"It's all your fault, you moron," Sal said.

"Watta we gonna do now, smart guy?" Joey asked.

"Well we can't stay here. The kid's gonna send somebody lookin for this one," Sal said, motioning to Thea.

"Yeah, we gotta move her. Or get rid of her." Joey added.

Thea's blood ran cold. Would they really kill her? She felt the need to try to reason with them.

"Look," she began, "the police already know who you are. And they know who you work for."

The two men looked up at her, anger in their faces.

"How?" Joey asked.

"I took pictures of you the night you attacked Jasper Collins. They know your names are Landolfi and Salvetti and you work for Corcoran. If you hurt me they'll come after you."

"Oh, wouldn't I like to hurt you, bitch," Joey leered.

"Joey, don't be no moron. She's right. But I betcha she's worth somethin to her family."

"I have no family," Thea said quietly, "they're all dead."

"What about Collins? He'd pay," Joey said to Sal.

"Why?" Thea asked. "I'm nothing to him. Just a friend."

"Does he fuck all his friends?" Joey asked. Thea blushed. Was their relationship that obvious?

"Just let me go," she pleaded.

"No way. Not till we talk to the boss," Sal replied as he walked in and tied her up again. She sank to the floor as they locked the door. She heard Sal tell Joey to walk to the house and call Corcoran, he'd stay here. And he'd better get another car from Rico or figure out how to move her. Thea hadn't eaten or gone to the bathroom, but she'd be damned if she'd ask anything of her captors until she had to. She was so angry and frustrated the tears streamed down her cheeks again. She tried to focus on Tori getting help, and hoped she'd be out of here soon.

TWENTY NINE

Tori drove at full speed but had no idea where she was going. She hoped she would see a policeman or he would see her and she could stop and tell him everything. She'd driven from the West End all the way to the roundabout at South Hill before that happened. The police car's lights came on as he saw the tan sedan with the dent in the fender, and Tori smashed the brake pedal, coming to a screeching halt and bumping her head on the steering wheel. She was already hysterical and crying when the policeman came to the car with his gun drawn. When he saw it was a young girl he put the gun away and pulled the door open.

"Miss Collins?" he asked. Tori couldn't speak, she just nodded her head up and down and bawled her eyes out.

THIRTY

Jas's lawyer Martin Kentwell had contacted Steve Ellis, a friend on the FBI's Organized Crime Taskforce. He told him the information he had from Chief Peter Moses on 'Sal' Salveti and Joey Landolfi. There was a high interest level on the part of the FBI, as they had been trying to bust the union's use of this rogue crime organization for about 18 months. This might be very useful. When Victoria Collins and Althea Garret were kidnapped Kentwell phoned his friend again.

"Steve, I have a serious problem," Martin began.

"What's up, Marty?"

"Jasper Collins daughter Victoria has been abducted. We think it's these characters I called you about late last week. They threatened to harm her and another woman, a friend of Jasper Collins, if we got the police or FBI involved. The police in the Caribbean are already involved, but I'm afraid if you go digging around in the union's business a red flag will go up. I don't want to see anything happen to them."

"I understand your concern, Marty, but it's too late. We've already begun talking to these guys. I'll pass the word about the kidnapping. Maybe we can dig something up that will help."

Martin Kentwell thanked his friend and hung up.

The FBIs first stop had been to Victor Sablan, to question him about his possible involvement with Corcoran, Salveti and Landolfi. Sablan had not yet been contacted regarding the kidnapping, so when he got the call from Jasper Collins' lawyer regarding his daughter's abduction he almost had a nervous breakdown. He thought about his own kids, and how he would feel in Collins' place. Then he realized if he let Corcoran get away with this that he would always have something on

Corcoran. He was scared to death of Corcoran or the mob wanting retribution or the mob thinking Sablan was involved in either Corcoran's windfall if the company sold or the demise of the union warehouse. If he turned state's evidence he could expose Corcoran and then Corcoran would take the heat for the warehouse closing. What's the worst that could happen? Corcoran could expose Sablan's brother's dirty secrets. And didn't this start because he wanted to protect Ted from a scandal? Well, fuck Ted, he was dead and if he hadn't been such a low life while he was alive Victor wouldn't have had to try to cover for him and protect the family name after his death. Being alive himself with no dealings with the mob outweighed a tarnished family name any day. The more he thought about it the clearer it all became. He called Steve Ellis at the FBI's Boston office and told him they needed to talk.

Corcoran's call from Joey Landolfi wasn't the worst possible news. The FBI had been sniffing around Sablan later the same day Corcoran had told Sal and Joey to pick up the Collins kid, and he had no way to contact them to call it off. Now the kid had escaped and he had no bargaining chip with Collins, but there was also nothing to stop Collins from continuing negotiations at his last offer price. If the deal fell through completely the union warehouse would remain intact. If the deal went through at the current price he'd have less money but he might be able to get away clean. He'd just continue to feign ignorance about the kidnapping and life would go on.

"Let the woman go and get the hell out of there," he told Joey.

"She knows who we are, boss."

"What do you mean? Did the Collins kid know?" Corcoran asked angrily.

"No, well, I dunno. The broad told the kid not to look at us, so she couldn't identify us. But the night we hit on Collins the bitch took pictures of us. She says the police know who we are, she said our names, yours too. She could identify us." Joey said.

"Kill her. Weigh her down and dump her in the ocean so they don't find her," Corcoran said quietly. He hung up the phone at the bar he used to receive calls from Sal and Joey at predetermined times. He was afraid the FBI might have bugged his home and office phones so he was extra careful about what he said on those lines. He knew he needed to liquidate all of his assets and flee. If the Collins kid led the FBI to him things would start to go south quickly. He needed to get out of the country now.

THIRTY ONE

Jas Collins was sitting with his head in his hands feeling more miserable than he'd ever felt in his life. Trevor and Jett were both asleep on chairs in the corner, Charles was in another office on the phone and Peter paced back and forth in front of the window. When Wilson Cooper entered Peter thought he'd have news of the whereabouts of Rico Costa's boat. Both he and Jas looked at him expectantly. He spoke to Jas.

"We have your daughter," he began as Jas quickly stood. Peter moved closer.

"What about Thea?" Peter asked.

"Yes, please," Jas added, "what about Thea?"

"No sign of her. Miss Collins was driving the tan vehicle with the creased fender. One of my officers stopped her. She was hysterical and couldn't speak. I directed him to take her directly to hospital, we'll meet them there."

Jas and Peter sprinted out the front door. The hospital was very nearby and they arrived just before the police car pulled up with Victoria in the back seat. Jas flew to his daughter who began crying again when she saw him.

"Daddy!" she wailed, "I've never been so scared!" She buried her face in her father's chest and sobbed. Tears were trickling from Jas eyes, his stony expression melting into relief and compassion. The girl was shaking and Peter was afraid she might be in shock. She had a lump forming on her forehead as well. He called for the doctor. A black woman appeared, as well as a nurse, and they attempted to escort Victoria inside. She refused to let go of her father.

"Victoria, I'm right here. We need to let the doctor look at you, darling. Then we need to speak with you, all right? Can you go with them? I'll be right beside you all the time." His voice was quiet and soothing, and she looked up at him through tearful eyes and nodded.

"Daddy, I'm afraid!"

"You don't need to be, darling. You're safe now," Jas said.

"No, no, I'm afraid for Thea! Daddy they hit her, I don't want them to hurt her anymore!"

Jas tried not to let his feelings show. He was sickened and angry, he wanted to lash out and hurt the men who did this, the men who hurt the woman he loved and scared his daughter half to death. He looked at Peter. His eyes betrayed his feelings and Peter nodded in silent agreement. Peter spoke to Tori as the doctor sat her on the gurney.

"Tori, can you tell me where they held you? Do you know where you were?"

"No! It was a dirt road off of another dirt road. The ocean was right there. Thea said it was calm, so it must have been the Caribbean side."

"How did you get away?" Peter asked.

"They came to take us to the ladies and to give us food. The ladies was a dust tip of a room out in back. They took me first, untied me and led me out."

"You were tied up?" Jas asked, the tension in his voice evident.

"Yes, arms and legs, but Thea untied me at night so I could sleep." Tori explained how Thea had maneuvered her arms in front and untied Tori's hands, and then retied her in the morning. "When I came back from the toilet they gave me a sandwich and a Coke. Then they took Thea out. I was so afraid. They knew she had helped you, Dad."

"How?" Jas asked.

"They made me angry and I... I blurted it out," she said, tears flowing again. "That's when he hit her."

"Victoria!" Jas said, incredulous. Peter placed his hand on Jas' shoulder to silence him.

"Tori, it's OK, we know you didn't mean it," Peter said. "How did he hit her?"

"I'm not sure. She told me not to look at them. She made me hide my eyes when they were around. I didn't see it, but I heard it, and she was tied up and couldn't keep her balance so she fell on me." The girl was sobbing now. Jas looked at Peter.

"She was trying to protect you," Peter said gently to Tori. "If you didn't see them there would be no reason for them to hurt you. You couldn't identify them." Tori nodded. Jas closed his eyes and shook his head.

"Tori, continue, please. What happened when they brought Thea outside?" Chief Cooper asked.

"One of them was such a creep. He had to carry her, I think her ankle is broken. She couldn't walk. He kept pawing at her and threatening to... Oh, God I hope he didn't! The other guy went outside to stop him from... touching her. I hit the guy by the door over the head with the bottle and I stole the car to get help!" Tori was overcome. The looks on Peter and Jas' faces disturbed Chief Cooper. He was afraid if either of the two men standing there got their hands on Salveti and Landolfi before his policemen did the perpetrators wouldn't live to see the inside of a jail cell. The doctor spoke.

"Gentlemen, this is obviously very distressing to this young woman. I need to take some x-rays, and you need to leave," she said sternly.

"Please, just one more question," Peter looked at the doctor imploringly. She nodded.

"Tori, when you finally got onto the tarmac road, do you remember what you saw?"

"Um, water, like a pond or something on the left. And a sign. Eclipse? On the right."

Peter looked at Chief Cooper.

"The West End. Possibly Barnes Bay. Let's go," Cooper said.

"All of you go," the doctor said. "I need to take care of this young lady."

Tori looked at her father with fear in her eyes.

"Victoria, I need to go now," Jas whispered. "You'll be safe here."

Just then Trevor and Jett bound in and came up beside her. Trevor took her hand. Tori looked relieved to see them.

"Where are Tim and Duncan?" she asked.

"Right here, Miss," Duncan said from the doorway.

"He'll be right here with you, darling," Jas said.

"Hurry Daddy. Please go get Thea!" she said, crying again. Jas hugged his daughter tightly, kissed her forehead and left.

THIRTY TWO

Thea sat against the wall with her eyes closed. The shack had to be 100 degrees and she had no water. She was exhausted, both physically and emotionally. It was probably unwise to tell them she knew who they were, but they might have killed her otherwise. They might kill her now because of it. Is this how her life would end, in a dirt floored shack being raped and murdered by two thugs that didn't mean to kidnap her in the first place? How ironic. After all she'd gone through to try and understand the deaths of her parents and Kip she felt like the butt of some big cosmic joke. One of her past lives must have been as a jurist during the Spanish Inquisition to deserve this fate. She hoped that if she were going to die that they would make it quick, although she knew she'd never go down without a fight.

Thea heard a car on the road, but she was too weak and tired to try to stand and look out. Her tethers made it so difficult for her to move. Joey Landolfi and a tall black man with long dreadlocks got out of the car and approached Sal. She could hear them talking but couldn't make out the words from where she sat. The door bounced open and the rush of air felt good on Thea's skin.

"What be wrong wit you, mon? It be a hundred degrees in here! You kill dis woman!" the black man said.

"It'd just save us the trouble," Joey muttered. Thea looked up. She could feel the adrenaline shoot through her body. "The boat's comin' for us out off the beach, but it can't get too close 'cause of the reef. One of the locals has a smaller one he's lettin us use to get out there." Joey said to Sal.

"Why don't you just leave me here, then," Thea said quietly. "Somebody will find me eventually. Just make a clean escape."

"No, babe, we got other plans for you. You're comin with us out to the boat. Maybe I'll get what I want from you after all, sweet stuff." Joey sneered as he pulled her up and wrapped his arm around her to carry her, grabbing her hair and pulling her face close to his. Thea closed her eyes and winced, from disgust as much as fear and pain. He threw her over his shoulder and carried her down toward the deserted beach.

THIRTY THREE

Chief Cooper, Peter, Jas and Tim were on their way from the Valley toward the West End when the radio sprang to life. Rico Costa's boat had been spotted leaving Little Bay traveling in the direction of Barnes Bay. Chief Cooper detoured from his course on the roundabout down to Sandy Ground, where he radioed for the police boat to be waiting.

"We shouldn't be far behind him. We'll catch up easily," Cooper offered. Jas and Peter were both ready to jump out of their skin. Jas kept trying to reassure himself that Thea would be all right. Cooper radioed his patrol cars to continue to Barnes Bay and look for a tin roofed shack at the end of a dirt road on the beach.

The men jumped into one of the waiting Boston Whalers and the young officer at the helm sped off toward Barnes Bay. Three officers and a pilot manned the second craft. Peter grabbed the binoculars and searched the boats in the distance for signs of Rico Costa. Jas looked at the nautical map at the helm and then tried to gauge their route from the landmarks on shore. He saw La Sirena and Malliouhana and realized they must be between Long Bay and Meads Bay, and would soon be approaching Barnes Bay. He, too, looked for the boat he'd seen in Thea's photograph.

Thea's captors had thrown her into the back of the small powerboat that arrived to take them to Rico's large fishing trawler. The black man who'd driven Joey back to the shed had taken his car and gone, and it was just Thea, Sal, Joey and the boat's driver making their way from shore. There were pleasure crafts about, so Sal had untied Thea's hands so as not to arouse suspicion. Joey was looking through binoculars in the vicinity around Rico's boat to make sure everything was

184

clear when he saw two medium sized crafts approaching at high speed in the distance.

"Sal, look at this!" he shouted over the noisy engine. Sal got up and threw the boat off balance as a water skiing boat passed close by. They hit the wake and the boat bounced hard. Thea took the opportunity in the confusion to slide off the back as the three men looked forward toward the trouble they were soon to encounter. By the time any of them turned around she was gone.

Thea had taken a deep breath before she hit the water and swam down and away, trying to stay underwater and get as far as she could before having to take another breath. Her legs were still tied, and one ankle was useless anyway, so her arms were her only means of propulsion. She wasn't sure if she was still swimming in the right direction. The flight response and the adrenaline were so strong that she thought she could swim the English Channel just then.

Sal and Joey were sure they were seeing police boats as they got closer to the Rico Suave. Joey realized they needed to dump their cargo before the police boat got close enough to see them. He pulled his gun and turned around to find Thea gone.

"Jesus Christ!" he screamed to no one in particular. "She's fucking gone!" Sal turned and looked, his jaw dropped open. They both scanned the water for her. The rough water that day made it difficult for them to see her, and they had already gone some distance before noticing her missing.

"She probably drowned," Sal shouted.

"That bitch, I hope so," Joey replied. He proceeded to unload his clip by peppering the waters behind them with gunshots.

Peter spotted the Rico Suave as well as the small craft approaching it. The pilot made a direct line toward the boat, and Chief Cooper pulled out a bullhorn. Both Peter and Cooper drew their weapons and Tim made Jas get down behind the protection of the helm. They watched the two men board the Rico Suave and the small boat they were in pulled away. Cooper signaled his other boat to go after the escaping small craft and question the driver. The pulled closer to the Rico Suave and Cooper shouted through the bullhorn.

"Rico Costa! Come out on deck. All passengers come out on deck, you are about to be boarded!"

Rico came out in typical Rico attitude, complaining about being harassed by the police just because he had a record. Sal and Joey stood behind him, hands on their concealed guns. The Whaler pulled up next to the Rico Suave and tied up. Rico saw the drawn police weapons and put his hands in the air.

"You two, hands up," Peter yelled. As they brought their hands up Jas could see them holding their guns, which were blocked from Peter and Chief Cooper's sight.

"Guns!" Jas yelled. Peter reacted quickly and took down Sal Salveti but Cooper had no clean shot with Rico Costa in the way. Joey Landolfi fired, hitting Peter Moses in the shoulder. Jas and Tim jumped onto the Rico Suave's deck, Jas tackling Joey Landolfi and pinning him to the ground, his gun skittering across the wooden boards. Tim grabbed the gun and pointed it at Joey just as Jas grabbed him by the throat.

"Where is she?" Jas snarled through clenched teeth.

"I don't know whatcha talkin about," Joey gasped.

"Let me remind you," Jas said as he slammed Joey's head against the deck several times.

"She's dead. Your pretty little bitch drowned. Too bad, cause we hadn't had any fun yet," Joey sneered. Jas felt a combination of fear, hatred, frustration and loss that he could not have imagined possible. He totally lost control. He began pounding his fists into Joey's face, beating him unconscious. It took two officers and Tim to pull Jas off of him. Joey was still alive, but barely. Jas and the police searched the vessel for any signs of Thea, but found none. They handcuffed Rico, Joey and the badly wounded Sal and commandeered the Rico Suave back toward Sandy Ground. Jas was returned to the police boat where he crouched next to Peter, who was bleeding but conscious. The look on Jas' face said it all. Peter closed his eyes for a moment.

"Jas, I'm sorry. It is obvious how you felt about each other. I'm so, so sorry," Peter whispered haltingly.

"Don't speak. Save your strength," Jas said, looking like he could easily break down.

Peter nodded.

When Thea surfaced for air the first time she was near enough to a channel marker to be able to hide behind it and get her bearings. She saw the boat, but luckily they weren't turning back for her. She watched Joey shoot his weapon into the water and shook with fear at the thought of being in the vicinity of the shots. She tried to untie her ankles, but couldn't seem to do it and keep her head above water. She looked toward shore, which seemed like a very long way, took a deep breath and dove under again, still trying to remain unnoticed. She came up for breath repeatedly and just kept focusing on shore.

Don't look back, she told herself, there's nothing you can do differently now, just go for it.

By the time she reached the shore she was a bit east of the place she'd been held captive. She dragged herself up onto the beach and under a sea grape branch and collapsed.

Chief Wilson Cooper radioed the men in the patrol car headed for Barnes Bay to continue to search for the shack. Jas looked up at him questioningly. Peter spoke quietly.

"Evidence," he said. Jas nodded, looking like he'd just been kicked again. Cooper spoke up.

"Not just evidence, Peter. We don't know if they actually took her into the boat. My men got nothing from the driver of their transport out to the Rico Suave. She could still be tied up in the shack where your daughter last saw her," he said, looking at Jas. Jas stood, looking toward shore, his hands in fists at his sides.

"Go," Peter said to him. Jas looked at Cooper, who signaled the other police boat over. Jas and Tim jumped aboard.

"Take these men with you to shore and search for the shack and Althea Garrett. I need to get Chief Moses to hospital," Cooper told his men. They set off toward shore and Cooper signaled his man to motor toward Sandy Ground. He could see Peter Moses was losing consciousness.

Jas squinted in the bright sun and wind as he looked toward shore. An active hurricane season had made the waters choppy in a usually calm bay. He ran through all the 'what ifs' in his mind. What if they killed her before they left? He'd have to steel himself to see her dead body. What if she had been aboard the boat and they killed her and dumped her overboard? He should be looking around for a body, he thought as his eyes roved over the water around him. They might never find a body if she floated out to sea. Could he hope she was alive? He wasn't a praying man, he'd always been spiritual in his own way, but he prayed to the Almighty, the universal energy, the goddess, or whoever really was running things to please help him now. Please let her be safe.

The police car pulled down the long dirt road just as the whaler reached shallow water. The men jumped out and all helped pull the vessel onto the beach. They could see the shack Victoria described a short distance away. They all approached, but Jas' heart ached as he saw the open door. The shack was empty. The police found the ropes the men had used to tie up Victoria, the empty coke bottle, cigarette butts and marijuana roaches but no Thea. The policeman in charge ordered his men to fan out, and especially to search the beach. If she'd been in the boat she might have washed up nearby. Jas and Tim had already headed toward the water. Tim wanted to stay close to Jas, but Jas ordered him to search the other direction. The beach was not long, and was interrupted by an outcropping of coral reef. There was no good way up and over it, so Jas waded into the water to go around. He looked out over the waves as well as along the reef, looking for what he was sure at this point would be her body. He was numb. He knew Victoria would take this badly, but he was heartsick, sure he'd lost the woman who could make him happy, the one he knew he could love. He pushed on, unsure why. He really just wanted to collapse or to drink himself into oblivion at that point. Another long stretch of beach lay before him. He could see a road on the other side of the fig and sea grape trees along the shore, and could see one of the policemen walking and searching the area. He must have been a quarter mile from the shack. A particularly large wave washed up on shore, reaching past the line of wet sand and almost to the trees. Jas noticed something move with the retreating wave. He saw Thea's lifeless legs, bound at the ankles, jutting out from under the low branches of a sea grape tree. He froze. He wasn't sure he was ready for what he would find. He yelled for the policeman who made his way through the vegetation to assist him.

He raised the branch and Jas lifted Thea into his arms. She was warm! He felt her neck. She had a strong pulse! She was alive!

"Oh, thank God, thank God," Jas repeated as he rocked her back and forth in his arms.

The policeman radioed his partner to drive the car up the road, and told the others to come and assist. It would be faster to get to hospital by car than by boat. They carried Thea to the cruiser and Jas held her in his arms as they maneuvered down the bumpy dirt road. His eyes welled up with tears as he looked at her. Her hair and clothes were wet and she was covered with sand. Her shoulders were sunburned. Her cheek was bruised all the way to her jaw where that monster had hit her. Her ankle was swollen.

The police had cut the ropes from her ankles, and what was left of her bandage wasn't worth keeping so he could see how bad it really was. It was nearly twice normal size.

She was breathing, and he kept talking to her, hoping she'd wake up. He didn't expect her reaction when she did.

Thea felt pain. Everything was fuzzy. Her head was fuzzy. She felt her ankle rubbing on something, her skin was hot, her head hurt and she was being held down. Trapped. She was afraid to open her eyes and look up. At who? Joey Landolfi? Oh, God they'd come back for her! They'd kill her for sure now.

"No!" she screamed as she sat up and grabbed the fencing separating the front seat from the back. She was trying to open the door and was flailing her other arm at her captor. The cop who was driving began to slow down and pull over while watching the back seat through his rearview mirror. Jas had been so surprised at her outburst that he hadn't had the presence of mind to try to restrain her. He shouted at her.

"Thea!"

She was still whimpering and trying to get out.

"Thea," he said again, gentler this time, as he grabbed her wrist. Her whole body tensed and she froze.

"Bloody hell, what have they done to you?" he said quietly as he gently touched her shoulder.

Jas? It was Jas? The relief that flooded her was palpable to everyone in the car. Her head dropped and she began to weep. Jas gently pulled her back to him and enfolded her in his arms, rubbing her back and kissing her forehead and eyes until she quieted.

"I've never been so scared," she whispered. "Even with everything."

"I know, it's alright now, darling. The police have them in custody."

"Tori, where's Tori?" she gasped.

"Victoria is at hospital. She has a bump on her head from her first island driving experience, but I don't think much else is wrong. She was frightened, too. Frightened for you, with good reason it seems."

Thea winced, thinking about Joey Landolfi touching her.

"Did he... touch you?" Jas asked.

"No," she whispered. "He threatened. He tried once but his partner stopped him."

They were quiet for a moment, Jas massaging her back and stroking her hair.

"Thea, I'm so sorry." Tears spilled down Jas' cheeks. He couldn't look at her. He was so ashamed that he couldn't protect her, or his daughter. He couldn't keep them safe. She looked up and with her thumb wiped his tears. She didn't know what to say to him.

THIRTY FOUR

Peter could hear someone calling him from what seemed a great distance, and through thick fog.

"Peter Moses," the woman's voice said, "Peter, can you hear me?"

It was a Caribbean accent, and a familiar voice. He tried to open his eyes and he murmured, but his mouth felt thick and gummy. He blinked and finally opened his eyes.

Everything hurt.

"Good! There you are. Peter, you've just come out of surgery. Do you remember what happened to you? You were shot in the shoulder."

"Yes," he mumbled. He looked up and saw the same doctor who had tended Victoria, only she was in scrubs and a surgical cap, her mask now down below her chin.

"I'm Dr. Livingston."

Peter chuckled, in spite of the pain.

"Yes, I get that a lot." She smiled at him. "The bullet did not hit the bone. You were very lucky. I repaired the muscle, and you'll need some therapy, but you'll be fine. How do you feel?"

"It hurts."

"Alright. I'll give you something for the pain." The doctor instructed the attending nurse to administer the medication. Peter felt a wave of dread go through him as he thought about Thea.

"Doctor?" Peter slurred. "My friend?" he tried to ask.

"Which one? You have a crowd in the waiting room."

"The woman they were looking for, Thea Garrett."

"Alive, safe and quite nearby. You'll be able to see her when you're moved to a room."

Peter's body visibly relaxed, he closed his eyes and let out a long breath.

"Rest now," the doctor said. "I'll let your friends know your condition." She smiled at him as she squeezed his hand.

Thea had her ankle x-rayed and was put into a cast. The doctor treated her for cuts and scrapes, sunburn and bruises, and gave her a mild medication for the pain. She'd be walking with crutches for a few weeks, but it would take longer than that to get over the trauma. She felt safe right now, with Jas, Tori, Jett and the others around her, but was concerned for Peter.

Dr. Livingston entered the waiting room and everyone looked up. Jett rose and went to the doctor.

"He's fine," she announced. The relief in the room was visible. Chief Cooper smiled broadly and patted Jett on the shoulder. "He'll be in recovery for a bit. When we move him to a room you may all see him. Miss Garrett, he's asked for you. I told him you were here and that you were well."

"Thank you, doctor." Thea said as the doctor departed. Her eyes welled up. Jas squeezed her hand. Jett came to the wheelchair she was forced to use and gave her a hug.

THIRTY FIVE

Jas took Tori and Trevor back to the yacht in the helicopter. He put Tori to bed and instructed Charles to contact him at the hospital if she needed anything. He then returned to tend to Thea, who was waiting to see Peter. Jas invited Jett to stay with them on the yacht until Peter could be released, at which point he offered to fly them both back to Nevis.

Thea welcomed the fresh clothing Jas brought her from the yacht, and he gingerly helped her change, trying to avoid her scraped and bruised flesh. She was exhausted when they were through. They had spoken little since her rescue, and what was spoken was mostly whispered. He communicated mostly by squeezing her hand, because he really didn't know what to say.

The nurse finally let Thea and Jett see Peter. He was sitting up in bed with a cast from shoulder to hand. He smiled broadly as Jett wheeled Thea in. Once next to the bed she stood on her good leg and leaned over him. She hugged him and he slid his usable arm around her.

"How can I ever thank you?" she said.

"You're alive. That's all the thanks I could possibly want. I can't imagine what this world would be like without you." Peter whispered. Thea smiled through her tears as she stroked his head and held his hand. Jett came around to the other side.

"I plan to torture you mercilessly in your incapacitated state," he said. Peter laughed.

"I will repay you ten fold when my cast is removed."

Jett smiled at his brother, leaned over and kissed the top of his head. The nurse came to the door with some administrative questions, and Jett volunteered to handle them for his brother. Thea and Peter were alone. Thea sat next to him on the bed.

"Did they hurt you, Thea?" he asked.

"No. Really, they didn't. They threatened to, and one guy got grabby, but the other one actually protected me. The ankle was broken when they put me in the car. They slammed the door on it, I'm told." Peter winced.

"They're both in custody," she said.

"They made it?" he asked, eyebrows raised.

"Yes. Why? What do you mean?"

"Well, I shot one. And Jas Collins beat the bloody hell out of the other."

"He did?"

"Yes, the one that shot me. The one that tried to have you. I watched from where I fell after I was shot. I thought Jas would kill him. It took 3 coppers and Tim to pull him off!"

Thea's eyes were wide.

"He loves you, you know." Peter said quietly. Thea just looked at him.

"I'm serious. I saw how he spoke about you. I saw how stricken he was when we thought you were gone. He's crazy about you. And he's a good man, Thea. He'd have given up everything to get you back."

Tears rolled down her cheeks again.

"And he lives in your world. He'll take care of you, I know he will. We developed all your film. I saw the photographs. I saw how you looked at him. You love him, too. Don't let him go Thea."

Thea reached over and hugged him again.

"So much has happened, Peter. I don't know what I'll do right now. I need to get over the shock of all this. And nothing has been promised."

"He hasn't told you he loves you?" Peter asked.

Thea shook her head in acknowledgement. "But we've made no plans. There's been no talk of the future."

"There will be. Mark my words," he whispered.

Just then Jett appeared at the door, with Jas Collins behind him.

"I told them you were indigent and would be sending them $1 per week for the rest of your life," Jett teased.

Jas walked over to Thea and reached around her to shake Peter's good hand.

"Glad to see you're on the mend," Jas said, smiling warily.

"Thank you, Jas. I'm glad Victoria and Thea are both safe. I'm sorry if I was harsh while we were..."

Jas interrupted.

"Don't be daft. You were under enormous pressure. I understand completely."

"And I want to thank you for your help on the boat. If you hadn't spotted the guns I might be dead now. You certainly restrained our perpetrator. How are your hands?" Peter asked, smiling. Thea grabbed Jas' knuckles and looked at the red, raw flesh. She let out a gasp.

"Sore," Jas whispered, grinning. "It was worth it."

Peter nodded.

"I think our Ms. Garrett needs some rest, so if you don't mind, I'd like to get her back to the yacht now," Jas said. Peter agreed, and told Jett to go as well as they could all use some sleep.

Peter had the nurse turn the lights down, and he gazed out the window at the darkening sky. He knew Thea was out of his life for good now. He just hoped she'd make the right decisions about her own. He could see Thea and Jas together. He would miss her, but it was all for the best. He sensed a presence in the doorway, and turned to look.

"Ah, Peter Moses, you are awake," the lovely lilting Caribbean accent whispered.

Peter watched as Dr. Livingston picked up his chart.

"Do you always dress like that when you're on duty?" he asked. She was wearing a red floral dress with straps that criss crossed in the back, and red high heels.

"I'm not on duty." She smiled as she looked up from the chart. "I was on my way to a party and I thought I'd check on you." She sat on the edge of the bed and took his pulse.

He studied her profile and he liked what he saw. Smooth, brown skin with an upturned nose, and large dark eyes. Her lips were painted the color of her dress. She was lovely. He hadn't noticed before while she was in her scrubs, hat and mask.

"You might be making my pulse race, doctor."

"Flirting. That's a good sign." She smiled at him.

"What is your Christian name, Dr. Livingston?"

"Sandra." She was still smiling. She rose and made a notation on his chart. "I will see you tomorrow, Peter Moses."

"I look forward to it, Sandra Livingston." She laughed upon hearing his words. He watched her walk out of the room and down the hall.

"Nice shoulders," he said to himself.

THIRTY SIX

Thea slept an exhausted sleep, thankfully with no dreams. Jas was close by, and whenever she moved he pulled her closer and wound his arms around her. She felt safe with him there. When she awoke she managed to disentangle herself from him and move gingerly to the sofa by the glass so she could look out over the Anguillan harbor.

She had a lot to think about. How badly would this set her back emotionally, psychologically? Would her ordeal manifest itself somehow? Would she need therapy again, and if so would she have to go home? And where was that? She let out a long sigh. Jas stirred.

"Thea? Are you alright?"

"Yeah. I'm fine." At least she was right now, as far as she knew. Jas joined her on the sofa.

"We haven't talked. Really talked, I mean," she said.

"I know."

"I guess there'll be a trial. I guess I'll have to testify."

Jas nodded.

"What about Tori?" she asked.

"Probably. Even though she didn't see them well she can identify their voices."

"How horrible. I wish she didn't have to go through that. I wish I could protect her from that," Thea mumbled.

He wanted to tell her that it was one of the reasons he loved her. The way she felt about Victoria. Instead he just took her hand and kissed it. He feared that if he took her into his life she'd be taken away from him. He was afraid he couldn't protect her. He loved her so much he would rather live life without her and know she was safe than risk having harm come to her again. His heart ached as he thought about it.

Thea sensed his distance. He had almost lost his daughter, and he no doubt had much on his mind. She wasn't ready for life in his world yet, so she was relieved the conversation hadn't gone that way.

They discussed the details of getting back to Nevis, and transporting Peter and Jett when the time came. Peter would be released soon. And they never discussed the future with each other.

THIRTY SEVEN

Life was getting back to normal on Nevis. Peter was able to resume light duty at the police station very quickly, and Jett made sure his brother was well looked after. Dr. Sandra Livingston took a very personal interest in Peter's case and was a frequent visitor, to the delight of Peter's family, friends and especially Thea. Thea thought they made a beautiful couple and she liked Sandra very much.

Thea found a counselor on St. Kitts. The short ferry ride made the sessions doable, and she felt she was working through some of her trauma before it got the best of her. Tori was in therapy back in London, and she e-mailed Thea weekly with her progress.

They had said a tearful goodbye when the Collinses left the Caribbean. Victoria was afraid she'd never see Thea again. So was Jasper, but he remained silent. Thea told Victoria how much she loved her, how they would always have a special bond after all they'd been through together, and how they were never more than an e-mail or a plane ride away. It was still difficult for Thea to say goodbye. She wasn't sure which was harder, Tori's kisses and tears or Jas' embrace and long, last look. Thea and Jas had been together only once more after the kidnapping. Their lovemaking was tender and gentle, each seeing something untouchable in the other's eyes. They held each other too tightly afterward; both knowing so much was left unsaid. Thea was now trying to get on with her life.

Charles Marston admonished Jas Collins almost daily for what Charles was sure was the biggest tactical error of Jas' stay on this mortal coil. Namely, letting Thea Garrett walk out of his life. Jas was miserable being without her. Charles made him more miserable every time he pointed out that Jas had never even given Thea the option, but just decided for himself she was better off without him. Jas once again immersed himself in work to try to suppress his feelings.

Thea's counselor worked long and hard to get at Thea's feelings. It was months before he got Thea to admit that the fear, the hurt and the anger were not all caused by the kidnapping. Thea's issues were all about abandonment. She had been abandoned by her parents, by Kip and now by Jas Collins. Only her parents and Kip were beyond her control, she could have addressed the issue with Jas and chose not to. She enabled him to abandon her by not facing the issue. She had done everything in her power to avoid it. To avoid telling him how much she loved him and Tori. Why? Fear that he would have eventually abandoned her anyway, and then she would have been a contributor to her own pain? Maybe. Fear that she would have been pushed back into the world that she felt overwhelmed by and had needed to escape? Perhaps. But she needed to overcome that fear and fast, because the trial was coming up and she needed to go to Boston to testify.

THIRTY EIGHT

Victor Sablan sang like a canary to the FBI, but the trial would still go forward as all allegedly guilty parties were still proclaiming their innocence. Joey Landolfi had even filed an assault charge against Jasper Collins. Thea was due to testify in Boston right around her birthday in October. She wondered if she would see Jas and Tori there. She asked Tori in an e-mail.

"They came and spoke to me here, in London," she wrote. "I think they call it a deposition? So now I don't have to go."

Thea was glad Tori wouldn't have to go through the pain of testifying, and actually be in a courtroom with those two thugs.

"Dad's supposed to be there, I think," Tori wrote. "I'm not sure when."

Thea knew she'd probably see Jas again at the trial, but tried not to think about how she'd feel. Her counselor told her that was not healthy.

Tori went into her father's office in their expansive Tudor castle, left to them by Tori's great grandfather. The office had once been a library, and Tori liked the dark walls and all the wonderful books. She'd curl up in front of the fireplace with a storybook as a little girl and listen to her father speak the language of business on the phone and with Charles. It was comforting to be there. Jas sat behind his big desk, reading glasses on, writing in his calendar. He looked up and smiled.

"Hello Darling. What brings you in here?" he asked.

"Dad, can we talk?"

"Of course. What about?" He took off his glasses and leaned back. Tori sat her hip on the edge of his desk.

"I just got an e-mail from Thea," she began.

In typical businessman's fashion Jas' face did not change, but he could feel his heart race at the sound of her name.

"How is she?" he asked, trying to sound calm.

"She's OK. Her cast is off and her ankle mended well. She's seeing a therapist, too. We usually compare notes."

Jas was amazed that Victoria had an ongoing relationship with Thea of which he wasn't even aware.

"How often do you write?" he asked off handedly.

"Oh, I don't know, several times a week. Sometimes we're both on line and we chat."

"Chat?" Jas's company had a web site and he surfed the Internet for business but had never gotten caught up in the personal interchange for anything other than professional correspondence. Tori explained it to him.

"Yeah. She's on my buddy list, so I can see if she's on line. Then I send her an instant message and she replies right away. Almost like having a phone conversation."

"You said she's in therapy, too?"

"Yes. That's what I wanted to ask you about." Tori paused. "Dad, I've been trying to be really good about not aggravating you and I do a lot of the things that Thea taught me. Don't misunderstand, I know it's hard being my father and I think you've been working really hard at it, too."

Jas was struck at how much like a grown up she was behaving, and amused at how much they had both learned from Thea about handling each other. Tori continued.

"And I don't want to start a row, but Dad, what happened? Really?"

"What do you mean?" Jas could feel his face flush.

"Dad, I'm not a baby." She gave him a condescending look. "You and Thea were really into each other. Everyone could see it."

Jas sighed. He rose and walked over to the window, not sure how to answer.

"Why is this coming up now?" he asked. "Did she ask about me?" He hoped she had.

"Well, not directly."

His heart sank.

"We were discussing therapy and we both had the same issue come up at the same time. I thought it was so cool that we seemed to be in sync, you know? But after we signed off I started thinking about it."

"What was the issue?" he asked.

"Abandonment," Tori said quietly. Jas turned to look at her.

"Please explain," he asked as he came over and took her hands. He led her to the leather sofa and sat facing her, still holding her hands.

"Well, in my case Dr. Firth said that I had issues with my mother walking out, and then you pulling away from me once I became a teenager, and then the kidnapping. He says the bad dreams I had might have been because I was afraid I would be abandoned, that you wouldn't have been able to find me, not because they would have hurt me."

"Oh, Darling. How awful." He hugged her.

"It's OK, Dad. You did find me and I just have to keep telling myself that I'm worthwhile and I'm lovable, and no one is going to abandon me. Thea gave me some really good affirmations to say every day."

"You are lovable, and you are worthwhile. You're so wonderful Victoria. How can I ever forgive myself for letting you think that you weren't?" Jas looked at her, holding her face in his hands.

"Dad, it's OK. Don't go all loopy on me or we'll all end up at Dr. Firth's."

Jas smiled.

"Besides, I wanted to talk about Thea. She said that she'd felt abandoned by her parents and Kip, her boyfriend. You know they all died?" she asked. He nodded.

"But what about us, Dad? Did we abandon her, too? What happened? We never even made plans to see her. Don't you care about her at all? I really thought you did."

Jas couldn't believe the insight and wisdom flowing from his child, even though her young face showed a child's confusion. He closed his eyes for a moment and took a deep breath. He rose from the sofa and walked back to the window. Such an adult question deserved an adult answer.

"Victoria, I love Thea very much," he paused. "But what I allowed to happen to her was unforgivable."

"What do you mean? You didn't do anything!"

"Because of who I am. I worry about you and your safety every day. I was so terrified when you were taken," he paused again. "I can't guarantee it won't happen again. And I can't ask someone to love me if I can't protect them."

"What about me, Dad? You love me and like you just said, there is no guarantee it won't happen again."

"You have no choice, Victoria. You're stuck with me, now aren't you?" It was more a statement than a question. He smiled sadly.

"Dad, the operative word here is CHOICE. You didn't give Thea one, did you? You didn't even ask if she wanted to be a part of our life, as mucked up as it might become. Bloody hell, no wonder she feels abandoned."

"Young lady, please mind your language."

"Sorry," she said sarcastically. They could both feel the tension rising.

"She wanted to know if we were coming for the trial," Tori continued. "I told her I didn't have to, but I thought you were going."

"What did she say?" he asked.

"That she was glad I didn't have to go through it, but that she would miss seeing me."

"Oh."

"I miss her."

"So do I," Jas whispered.

THIRTY NINE

Thea e-mailed Donny with her itinerary so he could pick her up at Logan airport in Boston. She'd be staying in town to be close to the Federal Court, but Donny agreed to take her to visit her parents and Kip's graves while she was home. Home. What an odd sound. She wasn't really sure where that was anymore. While she was on line booking her hotel she heard the musical notes of an instant message.

torious: Hello Thea

Thea smiled, typed a response and hit the send button.

tgar: Hi Tori! Isn't it a bit late for you to be up?

torious: I guess. I needed to ask you something.

tgar: What's up?

torious: Did you feel we abandoned you when we left?

Thea exhaled audibly. She thought for a moment before responding.

torious: Are you still there?

tgar: Yes. Pretty heavy stuff. Thinking about the answer …

torious: I'm sorry. Perhaps I shouldn't have asked.

Perhaps? Thea thought the wording didn't sound like Tori.

tgar: Your father and I left a lot of things unfinished. I didn't ask for anything and he didn't offer. So, no. I allowed what happened to happen, you didn't abandon me.

torious: Could it be different?

tgar: I think that's a conversation for your father and me.

There was a long pause before a reply came.

torious: Thea it's me. It's Jas.

Thea was floored. It had been 3 ½ months and no contact had been made between them.

tgar: Is Tori with you?

torious: No, she's asleep. Am I a horrible cad for not telling you it was me right off?

tgar: You're more of a horrible cad for not contacting me for 3 months.

torious: Would it help if I told you I haven't stopped thinking about you?

tgar: slightly

torious: I hate this! I can't tell if you're kidding!

tgar: then wait 5 minutes so I can get down to the greatroom and call me!

Thea ended her session, her heart thumping at her bold move. She shut down the computer and raced down the stairs.

Jas was stunned. He thought he would sign on as Victoria and just see if Thea was on line, not really expecting her to be. When they began their "chat" he hadn't intended to ask so serious a question. Knowing she was on the other end of the line was too much. He missed her so badly. Now she was asking him to call, presumably she didn't hate him for walking away. She even took some of the responsibility. He logged off, shut down and picked up the phone.

Thea slipped into Irene's office unnoticed and curled up on the wicker settee. She wondered if she'd imagined the whole e-mail exchange. Her shoulders were tense, she felt like she was in high school waiting for a boy to call. The phone rang.

"Figtree Inn," she answered in a melodious voice.

"I've never heard two words sound more beautiful," Jas responded.

Thea melted. She was on the verge of tears.

"Hi," she managed to eke out.

"How are you? How's the ankle... and the psyche?"

"Both are improving. I'm glad you called, you bastard."

"Nice talk. Are you glad?" he asked. "I wasn't sure you would be."

"Why?"

"I left things... badly" he replied.

"As did I," she said.

"Thea, I left so much unsaid." He began to ramble. "I was so afraid if I took you into my life I wouldn't be able to protect you. I'll never forgive myself for what happened to you."

"I forgive you," she said.

He was silent.

"And you know, this isn't just your decision. It's my life, I should have a say in it," she added.

"If I'd asked you to come to London with me. To be with me, would you have agreed?"

"Oh, Jas' I don't know. I'm really scared about leaving Nevis. Even going to Boston, which used to be home. I'm not sure where I belong."

"What does that mean for us?" he asked quietly. "You told me you loved me. Has that changed? Has my behavior changed it?"

"No. I still feel the same way about you, and about Tori. I'd love to have you in my life, but I don't know how to make that work."

"I miss you so much. I miss having my arms around you, I miss your scent. I miss burying my face in your hair. I ache to kiss you."

"Jas, this isn't a 1-900 number," she joked seductively.

"I don't want phone sex. I want you."

"Mmm, same here. I miss you," she whispered. "Why didn't we talk? Why did we both shut down?"

"I don't know. Fear, I guess. At least for me."

"What do you mean?" she asked.

"Thea, I told you what a revelation it was to feel love for someone after so long. Then to almost lose you. I convinced myself you would be safer if you weren't part of my life. I would rather know that you are safe and alive than in danger because of me. But I can't stand not having you near me," he said breathlessly. "Thea, I want to take care of you. Or at least try if you'll let me."

"I need to be able to take care of myself."

"Then let me be your safety net," he quickly responded.

They were both quiet for a moment.

"What happens now?" she asked.

"When do you go to Boston?"

She gave him her arrival date.

"Stay with me. Please. I'll be at the Ritz Carlton. I'll have a key for you at the desk if I haven't arrived yet."

Thea agreed.

"We'll figure this out, you know."

"Will we?" she asked.

"I love you, Thea."

They rang off.

FORTY

As the jet approached the runway at Logan Airport Thea could see the Boston skyline spread out before her. She had always considered it one of the most beautiful cities to fly into because of this view. Her heart beat faster, and she happily realized it was more from excited anticipation than from fear. Maybe it was OK to rejoin the real world after all.

Donny met her at the gate. She was thrilled at how happy he was to see her. He brought her a bouquet of lilies, and gave her a huge hug.

"I can't believe how much you've grown up, sweetie!" Thea said, holding him at arm's length. She needed to look up at him now. He looked like his father.

"Thea, you look awesome," he replied. "Great tan!"

She laughed and took his arm. They chatted about nothing and everything, and made their way to the short term parking lot to pick up Donny's car. He drove her into the city, and parked on Arlington Street, across from the Ritz.

"You're staying here?" he asked. She smiled.

"As a guest of a friend."

"A boyfriend?"

"Sort of." Thea looked at Donny with a guilty look on her face.

"Thea, Dad's dead. I don't expect you to be faithful to my dead father."

Thea hugged him. She knew he was a reasonable guy, but it was still hard to admit to him there was life after Kip.

Thea approached the front desk, Donny in tow. She asked after Jas Collins, and was told he had checked in, and left a key for her. She asked that the lilies be delivered to her room and put in water, dropped her bags for the bellman, and told them she'd be back for the key later.

"What should I tell Mr. Collins, Miss Garrett?" asked the concierge.

"Tell him I had a luncheon date with a very handsome man!" she replied, winking. Donny chuckled and the concierge smiled. She put her arm through Donny's and walked out into the brisk October sunshine.

An hour later the bellhop knocked at the suite's door and Charles answered.

"Miss Garrett's bags sir," he said. Charles let him in and looked behind him in the hallway in anticipation of seeing Thea, whom he missed almost as much as Jas did. The hall was empty.

"Where is she?" Charles asked, watching the bellhop put the vase of lilies on the desk in Thea's room.

"Oh, the concierge said she was having lunch with a handsome young man," he replied.

Charles smiled. Served Jas right for letting her get away. Jas came out of the sitting room and looked around.

"Is she here?" he asked Charles. Charles cleared his throat. The bellhop repeated the quote. Jas looked disturbed. Charles smiled again, hoping a lesson had been learned. Jas looked out the window, and could see down upon the public garden. He stared at the yellow and orange leaves and the wrought iron fence, watching the people on the street bundle themselves against the unseasonably chilly wind. Charles tipped the bellhop and went into the sitting room, leaving Jas alone. Jas had thought about nothing but Thea since they'd last spoken. He wasn't getting much business done, and was amazed at how preoccupied he'd become. He surmised that he really was in love. And now he was jealous. Again. Who was the handsome young man? He suddenly saw a woman walking through the gardens who seemed oblivious to the cold. The sun shone on her red hair and created what looked like an aura of warmth around her. She seemed so comfortable in her skin, so happy to be walking outdoors on this lovely, cold day. It was Thea. His skin flushed and his heart beat faster. She stopped to pet a dog on a leash and chatted with the walker. He could feel the warmth spread through him as he watched her smile and tilt her head as she laughed. How could he have possibly left her behind? It would be an eternity until she reached the suite, so he flew out of the room toward the elevator. Charles watched, bemused.

The attendant rushed Jas to the lobby, and he made his way out of the hotel wearing only a shirt, with nothing to brace him from the fall chill. The doorman stopped traffic so Jas could make his way toward the garden. He encountered Thea on the other side of the Arlington Street gate. Thea had turned north to see the sun shine off the State House dome. When she turned back toward the hotel she was swept up into Jas' arms totally unexpectedly, and cried out in surprise. He cut off her gasp with a kiss. He wrapped his arms around her and all the love he had for her flowed into that kiss, a desperate embrace that he never wanted to end. Thea relaxed into his arms, knowing she was home. She finally realized that home wasn't a place she could go to, or leave behind, but that it was a place within her that she carried wherever she felt loved. And she felt loved.

Dear Readers,

If you enjoyed *A Place Within Her* I hope you will leave a review at Amazon.com. I write these stories for all of you to enjoy, and the best way to spread the word is with your reviews. You have my undying gratitude.

As they say in the Caribbean, All the Best for the Day!

D.P. McHenry

About the Author

D.P. McHenry is a romance writer who makes her home in New England, and writes about the places she knows and loves. She is also a blogger, whose website is home to her rants on food, life, love and travel. Visit her at deborahdishes.com.

www.ingramcontent.com/pod-product-compliance
Lightning Source LLC
Chambersburg PA
CBHW060143130626
46556CB00006B/2474